THE WOOD

by
Elaine Sishton
and illustrated by Matthew Jeffery

HENDERSON
PUBLISHING LTD
©1996 HENDERSON PUBLISHING LTD

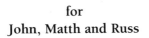

for
John, Matth and Russ

Chapter 1

Matthew Jardine kicked out at the nettles and overgrown bushes as he sped along the narrow track on his mountain bike. The wood he had cycled into was cool and dark. High branches from tall pines blocked out any hint of sunlight.

He hardly noticed the quietness that was now all around him. The air was very still. He crashed down the path. Brambles tore at his bare arms and legs, but he didn't feel them. He was too angry.

He shot along, not knowing where he was going. His head was down and he was blindly pedalling his bike forward, following the narrow path. Then suddenly the track stopped, or it had become overgrown, he wasn't sure which. What he did realise was that it would be impossible to go any further. He tried it for a while, standing up on the pedals out of the saddle, but it was like riding through custard, so he got off and pushed his bike forward. He wasn't ready to go back yet. No way

"Dangerous!" he muttered under his breath. "Everything I do lately is wrong. They just don't understand. Never mind me spoiling the holiday for them, what about them spoiling it for me? How was I to know the petrol would set alight like that? I was only trying to help them start the fire. It was Russell's fault as well.

But he doesn't get the blame, oh no. Just because he's younger. I try to explain things to them. They don't listen to me though. Just call me useless. It was only a little fire and we soon put it out. It's just not fair. I've a good mind not to go back at all. Then they'd be sorry."

He tore at some ferns and threw them angrily at a tree. It wasn't fair! Nothing went right for him at home. His parents were on at him night and day.

"Tidy your room, Matthew. Make a cup of tea, Matthew. Put your washing in the basket, Matthew. Don't play your music so loud, Matthew. Three bags full, Matthew!" he mimicked.

He was fed up with it. They didn't listen to what he had to say, so often he gave up trying. Then his parents would moan because he was too quiet. He couldn't win, no matter what he did.

He stopped suddenly as up ahead he saw a shaft of sunlight shining down on a small clearing. He pushed his bike towards it and decided to sit down for a rest. He was hot. Sweat was running down the sides of his face and he could feel it trickling down his back. His legs ached and looking at his watch he realised it had been well over an hour since he'd left the campsite where he was staying on holiday with his family. He lay his bike on the grass and sat down next to it. He breathed deeply, then lay back with his hands behind his head and looked up at the tree tops. The grass felt cool and springy under his legs. He meant to close his eyes for just a minute, to have a rest. But soon he was fast asleep.

It was almost dark when Matthew woke up. He stood up too quickly, rubbing his eyes and feeling dizzy. He looked around, wondering for a second where he was. He couldn't see the time on his watch, but he knew he'd been asleep for hours. Everything seemed different in the half-light.

He looked around for the pathway back to the campsite. The trouble was, there wasn't a path leading from the clearing, not even a gap in the grass to show him which way he'd come. Then it hit him: try as he might he couldn't remember the way back. He stood very still and listened. The silence seemed to rush to fill his ears. Not even the birds were singing. All he could hear was the sound of his own breathing.

Getting more frightened by the second, he held his breath. The blood started to thump in his head. He listened for some sound to follow, music, traffic, anything. He glanced around quickly, his eyes darting here and there. The wood was listening too. Everything was so still.

It was as if he were the last person left on earth. The silence was deafening.

Suddenly, he heard a twig snap behind him. He spun around and peered into the dark shadows of the wood. Nothing! He couldn't make out anything at all.

"Hello?" his voice sounded very thin and was

soon swallowed up by the silence. Another twig snapped, then another, splintering the stillness.

He panicked and turned, picking up his bike and pushing it, running as fast as he could into the wood. He wasn't even sure if he was going in the right direction but he ran for all he was worth. Branches lashed at his face and bushes whipped his legs. He was certain that something was following him, and whatever it was, it was getting closer. The trees bent down and reached out to grab him.

He ran even faster, his heart pounding in his ears. Gasping for breath his free arm thrashed wildly at the ferns and bushes. Then he found a path. Not a very wide one, but wide enough to ride his bike down. At least he could go faster. But where?

He pedalled frantically, not even sure he was going the right way. He sped on. Then it happened.

As he went flying over the handlebars, he calmly guessed that he'd hit a tree root. Something hard bashed his forehead as he went down. He lifted his hand to his face and felt a wet and sticky trickle. He knew he was bleeding before everything went black, blacker than even the darkness of the wood, and he passed out.

Chapter 2

Matthew lay on the ground, slightly surprised that he was still there. It wasn't dark any more. Strips of sunlight were breaking through the trees. He could hear the birds singing. His head was thumping. He didn't feel able to move and the earthy smell of the grass was strangely comforting.

He was cold, but decided that didn't matter. He felt that he didn't have to worry, he wouldn't have to move ever again if he didn't want to. He was comfortable lying still and besides, his head hurt if he moved it. He touched his eyebrow carefully. It was obviously swollen, but he thought that it had stopped bleeding.

With a great effort he turned himself over onto his back. As he looked up he made out a boy, about his own age and size standing over him. He was wearing blue jeans and a black T-shirt. He gasped, startled.

He tried to get up, but didn't make it, feeling sick and dizzy when he lifted his head. The boy stepped back looking almost afraid. He looked around him, then back to Matthew.

"Can you see me?" he asked.

"What?" frowned Matthew, shielding his eyes.

"Who are you?" said the clear voice above him. Matthew stared, unable to answer for a moment. "Who are you?" the boy repeated, "What are you doing in my wood?" Matthew pushed himself up into a sitting position and the boy squatted down to face him. Matthew peered into the boy's face. The first thing he noticed was a nasty cut running from the boy's temple to above his eye. It looked fresh and open and Matthew was surprised that there wasn't any blood.

"You've got a nasty cut there," Matthew pointed.

"So have you," the boy pointed back. "Have you got a hanky or a tissue, it's bleeding quite a bit. Must have been when you sat up."

"No," Matthew replied, fingering the cut.

The boy pushed a clean white handkerchief into his hand. Matthew dabbed the gash above his eye gingerly and cleaned up the cut and his hands as best he could with his spit.

"Thanks," said Matthew. They grinned at each other. "I'm Matt and I think I'm lost," he said, looking around and shrugging.

"My name's Ben. You're quite a way from the campsite, if that's where you're from," the boy said. "Here, hold that on your cut, it'll help stop the bleeding."

"Thanks. Yes, I came from the campsite. I left yesterday," Matthew said, holding the hanky firmly above his eye.

"Why? Why did you come to this part of the wood?"

"I got lost. I was angry at my parents. I ran away. They told me off about starting a fire..." Matthew stopped suddenly. "Mum and dad!

They'll be worried sick."

"I know all about parents. Does your mum fuss?"

"All the time, and my little brother's a pain!" Matthew answered smiling.

"My mum sewed my initials into my hankies! I lose them really easily see." Ben pointed at the corner of the hanky Matthew held to his eye.

"Now *that's* embarrassing!" Matthew shook his head and they both started to laugh. The sound rang out clear and sharp into the branches above them.

"I ran away once too. Trouble is..." Ben suddenly looked pensive. He stopped and looked up at the trees. "It wasn't fair. I only wanted to go into town with my friends. They wouldn't let me."

"What?" said Matthew. The boy continued, taking no notice of him.

"I never got to say goodbye," he mumbled.

"What do you mean?" asked Matthew.

"I think that's why I'm stuck here," he gestured around him, "in this wood."

"Stuck?"

"I can't leave."

"But you said you knew the way out." Matthew sounded worried.

"I do." Ben nodded and smiled. "Come on. I can take you so far."

Then he jogged away through the grass, leaving Matthew in a state of wonder. What on earth had he meant, I can take you so far?

"Wait!" called Matthew, not even sure if he could stand up. He jammed the handkerchief into his pocket. The boy came back.

"Sorry," he smiled. "But we have to go now. I haven't much time."

He helped Matthew to his feet.

"You okay?" he asked. Matthew nodded. He felt a bit wobbly if the truth be told, but he knew he could manage.

"How old are you?" Matthew asked him.

"Fourteen."

"Me too." Matthew smiled. "My bike! Wait!" he pointed to his bike lying on the grass.

"Don't worry. I'll bring it for you. You just bring yourself."

The boy picked it up and pushed it over to Matthew.

"It feels a bit like you look," the boy laughed. "Wobbly! You've buckled your front wheel, I'm afraid. Shame, neat bike."

"I hit a tree root, I think."

"Yep, that would've done it. Come on, follow me. We'll have to go quickly. I haven't much time."

"Why? Where have you got to be? What did you mean about being stuck?"

The boy didn't answer, but began to jog easily into the trees. Dizzy and feeling sick, Matthew made himself start forward. No matter how he tried, he just couldn't catch up with the boy running on ahead. He jogged on and on, always just in front. He looked back sometimes to make sure that Matthew could still see him. Then he would wave his arm for Matthew to follow. At last, Matthew felt he couldn't run another step. His head was reeling and the cut above his eye was bleeding badly. The handkerchief the boy had given him was soaked with blood.

"Wait, please!" he shouted, out of breath. The boy turned and waved, before running into the shadows of the trees. Matthew was all alone again. He'd lost sight of the boy. He tried to catch his breath and held onto his side to ease a terrible stitch. Where had he gone? Suddenly a voice shouted his name. It wasn't far off. Matthew recognised it.

"Dad?" he shouted, unable to believe his ears. "Dad! I'm here." He sank down to the floor of the forest, unable to go a step further. A policeman appeared from behind a tree, pushing Matthew's bike.

"Mr Jardine! Over here, sir. Is this your lad?" Matthew sighed with relief. He felt like crying, but gulped down the lump in his throat.

"Matthew?" His father was there at last. Running over, he bent down and grabbed Matthew into his arms holding him tightly. "We've been so worried."

"I'm sorry, Dad. I came off my bike," he half sobbed. "I got lost, you see."

"We found your bike a little way over there," his father said, gently helping him to his feet.

Then he turned to the policeman.

"Thank you, for helping me find my son. We're very grateful."

"He's a lucky lad, sir," the policeman replied kindly. "He wouldn't have been the first young 'un to be lost in this wood. There are acres and acres of forest here and you can go for miles without finding a path."

Matthew winced. His eye had suddenly become even more painful. The policeman peered at his face.

"Nasty cut there. Looks like a trip to the hospital for stitches, my lad."

Matthew's father turned him around and examined his forehead gently. Matthew pulled back. It was really hurting.

"It's all right Dad," he lied.

"We'll have to get you to hospital as soon as I've picked up your mum and Russell. Come on, we'll get your bike later."

"Where's the boy? Ben. The one that led me here," said Matthew suddenly. The men looked puzzled and shook their heads.

"No one came this way. We would've seen them," replied his father. "We found your bike in the clearing over there, we knew that you couldn't be far."

"He found me in the wood. He helped me and pushed my bike. I wouldn't have found my way back, if it hadn't been for him. He led me here."

His father looked at the policeman and they

both shook their heads.

"Must be the bump on the head, sir," whispered the policeman.

"Come on, now. Let's get you home. Your mother has been worried out of her mind." His father put an arm around him and helped him down the path.

A handkerchief soaked with blood fell out of Matthew's pocket and landed on the grass by the side of the path as they walked slowly to the car.

Chapter 3

It was a few days later before Matthew felt well enough to start thinking about what had happened to him in the wood. As far as his parents were concerned, he'd gone off in a temper, got lost, fallen off his bike and knocked himself out. His bike was still in for repair. It had needed a new front wheel. "You must have come a right cropper!" the man in the bike shop had said. Matthew had agreed with him and they had all laughed at his multi-coloured eye. But in the back of his mind, the memory of Ben still niggled. Matthew knew that he hadn't imagined him. He had been real enough at the time when he had led him out of the wood. The problem now was how could Matthew ever hope to track him down again? He was grateful for the help Ben had given him when he had come to his rescue. Funny that. One minute Matthew had been lying there trying to get his bearings - the next, he had bumped into Ben. Weird how he had turned up out of the blue like that, like some kind of guardian angel! He couldn't bear to think about what might have happened if Ben hadn't appeared. One thing was for sure, though, he would never have found his way out of that wood alone.

He sat now at the breakfast table, his head muddled with memories and recollections and unanswered questions. He was lightly touching the cut above his eye, which was still hurting like mad. The swelling was starting to go down and he had a beauty of a bruise coming out in all the colours of the rainbow.

"Don't touch, Matt!" his mum suddenly snapped him back to reality. "It'll never heal if you keep touching it like that."

"Sorry, Mum," said Matthew, chomping through his cornflakes once more. "This stuff's just a bit itchy, that's all."

"Shows it's healing," mumbled his dad.

"When I'm older I'm going to shave every hair off my body," Russell suddenly quipped.

"What's that got to do with anything?" snapped Matthew. It really was a pain sometimes having a little brother, even if he was only two years younger. Russell crossed his eyes at Matthew, so that his parents couldn't see.

"It's got lots to do with everything. I hate hair, to start off with. Plus...if I'd have fallen off *my* bike, they wouldn't have had to shave off *my* eyebrow before they could superglue me back together. Because..." Russell paused for breath, "there wouldn't have been an eyebrow there. See!" he crossed his eyes again.

"Shut up, stupid," said Matthew crossly. "You're giving me a headache."

"Can we go swimming today, Mum?" asked Russell, changing the subject.

"You can go with your dad, if you want. Matt can't go yet. He has to keep his cut dry for another few days. Remember?"

"Oh, yes. Never mind then. I wanted us all to go together." Russell caught his brother's eye and the two smiled briefly. Despite the usual bickering and arguing, deep down, when it mattered, they were good mates and enjoyed each other's company.

"I can't see why they didn't stitch that cut," their dad said, pouring another cup of tea.

"Less chance of scarring with this superglue, so they say. It seems to be closing up nicely." Matthew's mum made yet another trip over to his side to take a look at his eye. She kissed him lightly on the top of the head.

"Oh, Mum, get off!" he said.

"You love me to cuddle you," his mum teased.

"Poor likkle Mattie," whispered Russell.

"Shut up, flea brain!" Matthew answered.

"That's enough!" warned their dad and for a while all was quiet.

"I feel a lot better, actually," Matthew announced a little later. "Do you think it would be all right for me and Russ to go out over the field?"

His mum and dad looked at each other.

"Well..." answered his mum cautiously, "take it easy...and not for too long. I think you'll be okay. If you don't feel well you're to come straight back, do you hear?"

"Okay, Mum. Thanks. Are you coming, Russ?"

Russ leapt up, nodding his head, his mouth full of food. He loved it when his big brother included him in his plans.

16

"Sit yourself back down and finish eating first! You'll choke, running around like that," ordered his dad. Russell sat down again and bolted through his breakfast. Matthew and his mum started laughing, so he exaggerated the action to make them laugh even more.

"He looks like a camel on fast forward," giggled his mum. "Now don't forget, no overdoing it. Don't go too far. Be sensible, Russell, we all know what you're like."

"Yes, Mum," Russell chimed. The two of them had almost got to the caravan door and made their escape when someone knocked on it. Matthew and Russell looked at each other. Russell screwed up his face with a certain knowledge of who it was. He opened the door.

"Oh, hello," he said. He had been right. It was Sophie. She was the campsite owner's daughter and she was twelve years old, the same age as Russell. She had latched onto them and had tagged along with them for a few days before Matthew's accident. Now she was back! What a surprise - who wants a girl tagging along anyway?

"Hello," answered Sophie, smiling at them both. "How are you, Matt? I thought I'd give it a few days before I popped round. Mum said you'd be feeling quite poorly with a bump like that. Nice eye."

"Is that Sophie?" Russell's mum called. "Ask her in, Russ."

Russ smiled begrudgingly and said very

THE WOOD

17

reluctantly, "Come in then." Everyone said their hellos.

"I'm surprised to see you up, Matt," she said cheerfully.

"I'm feeling much better now, thanks. I heal quickly," he replied.

"Good. We were worried that you may have cut your holiday short and gone straight back home after your fall. We're glad you decided to stay," she said.

"We nearly did go home," replied Matthew's dad. "But Matt bounced back as good as new and we all agreed to stay on and finish our holiday. After all, we're here for another two weeks. Matt will be fully recovered by the time we get back and his bruise will have settled down nicely.

"I was wondering if you were well enough for a walk. Well, that's if you and Russ want to come, that is. And if you're not going out with your mum and dad of course."

"We did all our visiting at the start of the hols, Sophie. The lads are all yours, if you want them," laughed their mum. The brothers exchanged mutual glances of dismay; but Matthew knew how lonely Sophie was, living on a farm, in a little village with hardly anyone else to go round with. She was obviously grateful for some good company at last. Russell read Matthew's mind and surprised them all by saying, "We're just off over the field. You can come, if you like, I suppose."

Sophie's face lit up.

"Thanks!" she beamed.

Matthew and Russell grabbed their jackets and struggled with their trainers.

"We'll be back for lunch at about one," called Matthew.

"Okay, see you all later," his mum called from the kitchen. Then they were gone. She watched the three of them walk over towards the field and disappear into the distance.

It was the first time Matthew had been out for a proper walk for a few days. He breathed in the fresh air, inhaling deeply, until it filled his lungs. Cold clean air - it felt brilliant. They walked over the field towards the trees that marked the beginnings of Wendles Wood.

"Where are we going, then?" asked Sophie.

"To the den," Matthew replied quietly, "I want to talk to you both about something. I've got a feeling I'm going to need your help."

Chapter 4

When they had been together the first few days of the holiday, they had all set to and built a hide-out just inside Wendles Wood. It was nothing much, just a clearing in amongst some bushes. There was enough room for them all to sit and it was sheltered from the wind, and so far had proved rainproof. They had built up the sides and made a roof by adding fallen branches, twigs and leaves. Now it was well camouflaged and comfortable...and provided them with a mutual meeting ground, away from parental eyes.

When they were in the wood, they realised they had almost hidden the den too well. It took them a few minutes to find it. Once inside they all sat down, then Russell and Sophie both turned expectantly to Matthew.

"What's up then, Matt?" asked Russell.

"Well, I've got a feeling that you may not believe what I'm going to say to you. So, I don't know whether to tell you or not."

Russell and Sophie looked at each other, wide-eyed.

· "Well hurry up! Put us out of our misery then," said Sophie, trying to lighten the atmosphere. As if Matthew's tone of voice wasn't bad enough - the den added to the eerie feeling. Inside the wood a stillness hung in the air above them. Not a pleasant stillness - rather a feeling of discomfort and tension. Sophie laughed with uncertainty.

"Come on, Matt. You might as well tell us now." She tried to hide her unease.

"Yes, come on. You can't start something like that and not finish it," said Russell. "You're so melodramatic, Matt."

So Matthew told them about what had happened the day of his accident. He told them about how he'd got lost, fallen from his bike and had been knocked out. Then he went into a detailed description of his cut eye, of how much blood there had been and how the wound was gaping open. He began to tell them about the meeting with Ben, about the strange things Ben had said during their conversation and how Ben had jogged away into the wood and eventually had led him to safety.

Sophie was looking down at the ground and had become unusually quiet. Russell laughed shortly when Matthew had finished.

"Dad never said anything about a boy leading you out. He said they found you at the edge of Wendles Wood. Why didn't you tell Dad about this so called friend? This Ben? You're fibbing, that's why," mocked Russell.

"I did tell Dad and the policeman," replied Matthew, "but they said I was imagining things, because of the bump on my head."

"Well, perhaps they were right. Perhaps you did imagine it all," said Russell. "You've always been a bit funny in the head, anyway," he added to try and lighten everyone's mood a little. Matthew was not amused. What he had seen had been as clear as crystal.

"I know I didn't imagine it. He was there, I'm sure of it and I don't know where he went. He didn't seem to be lost, so he must live close by. I want you two to try and help me find him. To say thank you."

Sophie, who had been quiet for a while, suddenly spoke. Her voice was tentative - a whisper, and it seemed to the brothers that she had become quite pale.

"What did he look like, this Ben?" she asked quietly.

"Oh, about my size. He said he was fourteen, too, the same as me. Um, blonde hair, very deep blue eyes. Good runner, oh yes, and he knew about your campsite. Had jeans and a black T-shirt on. Said his mother fussed a lot, too. We had a laugh about that," answered Matthew.

"His mum as well?" laughed Russell. Then he noticed Sophie's face and shut up again.

"What's up, Sophie? You look like you've seen a ghost," said Russell.

"No, I haven't. But I think *you* might have, Matt."

Matthew wanted to laugh out loud, so did Russell, but the look on Sophie's face told them both that she was deadly serious. They thought, for a moment, that she was going to cry.

"What are you jibbering on about?" said Russell.

22

"I'm talking about Ben," she said.

"Who? The Ben I saw. You know him, then?" Matthew said.

"Correction, I knew him. His name was Ben Walker. He and his family stayed at our campsite for a few years on the trot. Then, about three years ago...er, yes, I was nine when it happened...Ben went missing. He was fourteen. People thought he'd been kidnapped or murdered or something. We later found out that he went off into the woods in a filthy mood after a row with his mum and dad. Anyway, he was never seen again. His body was never recovered. The police searched for days, scoured the whole of the wood. They still believe he's here, though, somewhere."

"I think that's just your imagination working overtime Sophie. The boy who Matt saw was probably just another holiday-maker," said Russell.

"Well, Ben certainly fits the description Matt's just given. He was fourteen when he went missing. Blonde hair, deep blue eyes. Lovely deep blue eyes," she said dreamily.

"Oh, yuk! No wonder you wish Matt had really seen Ben!" Russell pretended to put his fingers down his throat.

"Be quiet!" hissed Matthew.

"I thought he was great. Had a big crush on him. He was a good runner, too. He ran cross-country for his county," Sophie carried on.

"That would explain a lot of things that have

been bothering me. Those strange things he said. Very weird," nodded Matthew.

"It also means that you have to believe in ghosts. No way! I certainly don't. You have no proof - just silly speculation. What a load of rubbish," scoffed Russell.

"I think it's possible," said Sophie. "But Russ is right, you have no proof."

"Wait a minute," Matthew said thoughtfully, suddenly realising something. "I may have proof after all. The hanky!"

"Hanky? What hanky?" asked Russell.

"Ben gave me his hanky, to stop the cut above my eye from bleeding too much."

"So where is it then?" asked his brother.

"I don't know. It isn't in the caravan. Mum would have noticed it. It was soaked with blood. It wasn't in any of my pockets, either."

"You must have dropped it then, when your dad and the policeman found you. You must have dropped it around there somewhere," said Sophie, sensibly reasoning it out.

"This is crazy!" laughed Russell. "I can't believe we're talking like this. There's no such things as ghosts, well, not around here anyway. If there are, they certainly wouldn't talk to you."

"Mum said they found you on the other side of the wood, near Stile Copse. We could go now! We'd be back well before one o'clock. I know the short cuts." Sophie spoke directly to Matthew, ignoring Russell.

"No, we can't. We may not be back in time.

Besides, Mum said Matt wasn't to overdo it," Russell said sulkily.

"Are you sure you can find the way, Sophie?" Matthew asked, although he had complete faith in her. Sophie knew that wood like it was the back of her hand. It was as familiar to her as the farm and she knew every path and turning. Her parents had always taken her into the wood, ever since she was a little girl. She had happy memories of childhood picnics there and now Wendles Wood had become a friend to her.

"Hello! Hello! Is anyone listening to me?" shouted Russell.

"That was another thing that puzzled me about Ben's disappearance, well death, I suppose, although it's never been proven. He knew this wood almost as well as I do. He couldn't have got lost, like they said he had."

The three of them walked through the wood, with Russell following reluctantly behind. He was kicking at clumps of grass and stifling an unwanted feeling of anxiety. All this ghosty talk was unsettling.

They stopped every now and then to look at some unusual flower, rare fungus, or old tree and eventually Russell caught them up and walked with them.

After about half an hour Sophie pointed in front of them,

"Stile Copse is just ahead," she said. "Do you recognise anything, Matt?"

"Afraid not. Not yet anyway. Let's go a bit

further." Matthew frowned, looking around for some familiar sign. They walked on.

"We're nearly at the road," said Sophie.

"This hanky, even if we do find it, it won't prove anything," said Russell.

"Yes, it will, Russ. Ben's mum was very fussy. She sewed his initials into the corner of his handkerchiefs, because he lost so many of them. He told me."

"So?"

"Well, I only knew his name was Ben. It was Sophie who told me it might be Ben Walker."

The brothers walked together, talking.

"I still don't..." Russell began.

"Wait a minute!" called Sophie, a little way behind them. "Look!"

They ran back. Sophie was standing over something crumpled. It looked like a stained brown paper bag, or so Russell thought.

"Well done, Sophie, that looks like it."

Matthew picked it up and shook it. It was wet and soggy, stained with old blood and covered with insects. The three of them gathered around, by now all quite excited. Matthew straightened out the hanky and pulled at one corner. There, quite clearly, neatly embroidered by someone's careful hand, were the initials BW.

"Ben Walker," said Russell.

26

Chapter 5

The three of them stood for some time, just looking at the handkerchief, wondering what to do next. It was certainly proof, proof that Ben existed and that Matthew hadn't just imagined him. They half expected something weird to happen. Perhaps Ben would appear like a ghostly ghoul. But he didn't, no matter how often they glanced over their shoulders or around the backs of the trees.

At last Russell spoke, interrupting the deafening silence of the wood.

"Well, what do we do now?" he said. Both he and Sophie looked to Matthew for an answer.

"I'm not sure," he mumbled. "Let's think about it after lunch. Come on, I'm starving. We've got to be back by one o'clock, or else! Come on, Mum will be worried." The others stood open-mouthed at his answer. It was as though a weight had been lifted from him, now that they had found the hanky.

"Unbe...lievable!" gasped Russell. "Only you could think of your fat stomach at a time like this!"

But they knew Matthew was right. There was nothing they could do straight away. They had to make a plan. So they walked back to the campsite with Ben's handkerchief, hardly saying a word to one another. They were in the wood where Ben had disappeared. His body may be somewhere near. They expected to see him at every step. They spun round more than once as they imagined the spooky snap of a twig cracking behind them, but to their relief, they saw nothing.

They got back to the campsite just before one o'clock.

"See, told you I'd get you back in time," Sophie said. "See you after lunch, then?" she asked hopefully.

Matthew answered quickly, "Yes, but don't tell anyone about what we found. Not a word. Not even to your mum or dad. Nor you, Russ."

Russell shook his head and Matthew realised he had no intention of telling anyone. Matthew went on, "We're going back to the wood this afternoon. I want to try to find Ben again. Do you still want to come?"

"Course!" smiled Sophie and ran off towards the farmhouse.

The boys exchanged glances.

"Why have you asked her to come?" asked Russell.

"Because she knows that wood better than anyone. You haven't got a problem with that, have you?" said Matthew.

"No, but you have. She fancies you, you know. I can tell by the way she looks adoringly into your big brown eyes."

Russell pushed Matthew playfully. "Slushy, like."

"Get lost," replied Matthew as they opened

the caravan door to the tempting smell of bacon sandwiches.

It was three o'clock before the three of them were seen walking back towards the wood. Mrs Jardine had been very reluctant to let Matthew go out again, but he had managed to put her mind at rest.

"Where are we going?" asked Sophie.

"Into the middle of the wood. We're going to try to find Ben Walker," Matthew replied.

"What do we do when, sorry, I mean if, we find him?" asked Russell.

"I don't know," Matthew said impatiently. "Let's just try to find him first, eh?"

"My aunt would be able to find him," Sophie piped up. Russell raised his eyes to the heavens.

"What makes you say something as daft as that?" he asked.

"She's the local medium. In the village she's..."

"A what?" asked Russell. "What's a medium? It sounds like some kind of steak! Medium please, waiter!"

Sophie gave him a dirty look and spoke directly to Matthew, who was trying not to smile.

"She's like Whoopi Goldberg in *Ghost*. She's able to talk to the spirits of people who have passed away."

"Lovely!" Russell scrunched up his face.

"We may need to speak to her if we can't find Ben. Do you think she'd help us?" Matthew said, his voice going suddenly quiet as they walked into the eerie stillness of the wood.

"She's a bit mad, though," added Sophie.

"Surprise, surprise," joked Russell. "What's she called? Wanda Witch?"

Sophie leapt at Russell, but he was ready and jumped sideways before he ran off around some bushes.

"Come back and fight me, you coward!" shouted Sophie. Russell squealed in mock horror and ran faster with Sophie hot on his heels, her arms outstretched to catch him.

"Come back, you two," called Matthew, smiling. He knew there was no chance of losing them. Sophie knew the woods too well, and Russell? Well, Russell's voice was loud enough to be heard for miles.

Matthew walked after them, following the racket they were making.

"Hello," a voice said, just over his shoulder. He spun around on his heels, startled. He thought Russell had doubled back and was trying to frighten him. But it wasn't Russell. It was Ben.

"I was looking for you," Matthew said. "I wanted to say thanks for saving my life."

"That's okay," Ben shrugged. "Glad I could help. Besides, you would've done the same for me." He walked closer to Matthew and examined his cut. "It's healing nicely. Brilliant bruise!"

"Yep, still hurts a bit when I fiddle about with it," said Matthew. "What about yours?" he pointed to the white gash above Ben's eye.

"No, that's never hurt me. It won't heal

though. I don't suppose it ever will now."

"No, you're probably right," Matthew said simply.

"How come you can see me?" Ben asked. Matthew was a little taken aback, suddenly realising that he was talking to someone who wasn't alive any more. Ben continued, "You're the first person to be able to see me since I've been stuck here, if you know what I mean."

"I *think* I know," said Matthew, very matter of factly and wondering why he wasn't afraid. "You're dead, aren't you? You're a ghost."

"It seems that way," said Ben. "But I don't seem to be going anywhere. I'm stuck here, in the wood. I can't go any further than its boundaries. I'm beginning to think that I'll be here forever in a kind of limbo. I don't know what I have to do to get out and carry on."

"Carry on?" echoed Matthew.

"Yes, I've a feeling I've got somewhere to go, but..."

"I'd like to help, if I can. My brother is close by, with our friend. I'll call them," said Matthew, looking around for Russell and Sophie.

"I don't think they'll be able to see me," frowned Ben.

"Wait and see. You may as well give it a try," said Matthew.

"No, I'll meet you again. Come back to the wood and we'll talk. You will come back, won't you? I need your help to get out of this place." Ben began to jog away, then he called, "By the way, who won the Rugby World Cup this year?"

"South Africa," answered Matthew.

"What about England?" asked Ben.

"Nowhere near! We were put out by New Zealand. Wait! I can hear my brother now."

"So can I!" shouted Ben as he jogged away, waving.

Matthew waved back just as Russell and Sophie came into view, wrestling. Sophie was holding Russell in a headlock and he was pretending to be strangled.

"Who are you waving at?" asked Sophie, releasing her hold on Russell. He rubbed his neck.

"Ben," said Matthew. "He was here. Did you see him?"

"No. What did he say?" asked Russell, peering in the direction he'd seen Matthew waving.

"He needs our help, Russ, and we're going to give it to him."

"How?" asked Russ and Sophie together.

"I'm not sure yet. I think we'll pay your aunt a visit for starters."

"Well, what else did he say?" asked Russell.

"He asked who'd won the Rugby World Cup this year," smiled Matthew, as they headed back towards the campsite.

"South Africa, wasn't it? I could have told him that!" mumbled Russell to himself.

Chapter 6

Matthew was back in the wood. It was late afternoon and he didn't recognise where he was. He began to wish Sophie was there with him. She would have known exactly where they were.

A mist hung over the tops of the trees as he stood and looked around, trying to pinpoint some landmark. A dead tree, a clump of flowers, anything that could give him a clue as to his whereabouts.

But there was nothing familiar. Nothing at all. He began to walk along one of the paths, glancing around and looking over his shoulder constantly.

The air was as still and as silent as the mist. The smell of earth and peat was stronger than usual and filtered into his nostrils. Matthew had been aware of the smell every time he had entered the wood, but never as strong as this. All the time the silence of the wood enveloped him like an invisible cloak, shielding him from the outside world

He walked on, unsure of the direction he was going, or even of the way he had come. He was lost.

It was beginning to get colder. He shivered in the half-light and stopped to look around once more. Nothing. Where was Ben? Ben would surely find him soon. Find him and lead him safely out of the wood, where his family would be waiting.

A twig snapped somewhere behind him and he spun round quickly.

"Ben?" he said, but no sound came out of his mouth. There was nothing. No sound, no sign of Ben. Fear crept over him once more, up from his toes until it clutched at his heart like an ice cold hand. Matthew found it almost impossible to breathe. He tried to shout out for help, but couldn't. His voice had frozen in his throat.

The mist around him seemed to close in, choking and blinding. It rolled and swirled around, thicker and thicker, until it was impossible to see more than a few feet in front of his face. Then he tried to move, to run, but couldn't. His whole body appeared to be useless, paralysed. He pumped his arms, trying to get his whole body moving, but it was as if someone had switched him to slow motion.

He looked down at his feet. To his horror, he couldn't see them. They had been swallowed up by the earth. He was standing now, embedded in the ground. He was sure of it. He opened his mouth to scream, but again his scream was silent. He felt cold sweat trickle down his back and it was running down the sides of his face. He tried desperately to wipe it off, but his hands wouldn't move.

Suddenly, there was a noise behind him. He looked around frantically, hoping it was someone who could help him. Hoping it was Ben.

The mist slowly cleared and in so doing

released his body. He could move again. He turned in the direction of the noise, stumbled forward, then caught himself. He stood upright and saw the outline of two figures approaching him. They were both laughing. He heard the laughter first, before they broke through the mist.

"Help me!" he shouted. "I'm lost."

The figures approached, but made no sign that they had either seen or heard him.

"Help!" He shouted louder. Still they didn't answer, or even look his way. Then he noticed that they were both carrying guns.

He was paralysed once more, unable to move or to run away. Every second the figures came closer, but no matter how close they came, he could not see their faces. They were both men, he was pretty sure of that. He could tell by the way they walked and carried themselves. Why couldn't he see their faces though?

They were now very close to him, only a few feet away. Yet still they made no indication that they had seen him. They were looking up at the trees. They were pointing upwards and laughing, horrible, hollow laughing that echoed around the trees and rang in Matthew's ears.

Then Matthew saw them raise their guns. They were pointing straight at him!

"Wait!" he called desperately. He heard the gunshots and closed his eyes tightly.

"I'm dead!" he remembered thinking. After a few seconds he opened his eyes and looked down at his body. He wasn't hurt. He was okay. How? He looked over to where the figures had been standing, in time to see them walking away from him into the mist. They carried their guns over their shoulders and he could still hear them laughing.

He thought about shouting after them to ask them what they thought they were doing, frightening people like that. His mum would have. But a sound above him made him look up.

A large bird was dropping through the air towards him. It caught on branches and twigs, crunching and cracking them on the way down. Matthew watched it, almost in a trance. It seemed to fall in slow motion - gracefully - heavily. Dead weight. Matthew knew it was dead even before it hit the ground at his feet. It thudded down before him, raising dead leaves in its wake. He stood for what seemed like a long time just staring down at it. It was a big bird with beautifully coloured plumage, he could tell that even in the half-light. Purples and blues swirled together over gossamer soft downy feathers. He hadn't got a clue what kind of bird it was. Birds had never really interested him that much. But this one was beautiful.

He bent down at last to take a closer look. He prodded it gently with one finger, then placed his hand over the folded wings. It was still warm, and it was very, very soft. He stroked it, then noticed with shock that his hand was covered with blood. The bird was bleeding and the blood was all over his hand. He reeled back. It had been shot twice, he could see that now. Once through its body and once neatly through its head.

The blood oozed through the feathers. He looked at his hands. The blood was muddy on his fingers. It was everywhere.

The two men had shot this bird for no reason. They'd shot it, let it fall with a thwack on the ground and left it. They'd taken its life for a laugh.

He tried to wipe his hands on clumps of grass around him, but the blood wouldn't come off. Both his hands were stained with it. He stood up, looking down at the dead bird, anger welling up inside him. They'd had no right to do this, no right at all. He shouted out a deafening, "No!". His cry splintered the silence of the wood and set the birds off flapping above him. Then he was off and running in the direction that the figures had taken. He would catch them. But then what? What would he do? He didn't care. He would give them a piece of his mind, for a start.

He ran with all his might but his legs began to feel like lead. He felt as though he was tied to a fully stretched piece of elastic. He was getting nowhere fast.

The blood still stained his hands. He didn't know where it had all come from and he couldn't rub it off. He began to think that he himself was bleeding.

Suddenly he broke free of the mist into a clearing. There were the two men. They were sitting on tree stumps and around their feet lay the bodies of different dead birds. They lay like ritual sacrifices. Matthew stood aghast.

"No!" he shouted again and began to run towards them. The faceless figures looked up and saw him running towards them. One of them raised a gun to his shoulder and aimed straight for him.

"No!" Matthew shouted again. He sat suddenly bolt upright and came face to face with his brother.

"What's the matter with you?" asked Russell. "You've been making a right racket. Mumbling and shouting and rubbing your hands on your quilt, are you okay?"

Matthew sat shivering, his hair stuck to his forehead with cold sweat. He looked around frantically.

"It's all right, Russ," he finally whispered, "Just a dream."

"Must've been a corker!" mumbled Russell.

"Pretty bad," answered Matthew, "it seemed so real."

He turned over but it was a while before he managed to drop back off into a fitful sleep.

Chapter 7

Sophie came round to their caravan just after breakfast the next morning.

"Thought I'd call for Matt and Russ," she said cheerily to Mrs Jardine as she opened the caravan door.

"Hang on a minute, Sophie, I'll just hurry them along. Matt's still watching the TV in his boxer shorts! Come in, anyway. It'll embarrass him like mad. Might even get him to get dressed, you never know. I sometimes think he's rooted to that spot in front of the TV."

Sophie walked into the lounge, giggling. Matthew shot up like a scalded cat, from where he'd been lazily lounging on the sofa, and disappeared into his bedroom, shouting, "Mum!" very angrily.

Sophie waited. After a while Matthew and Russell came into the lounge fully dressed.

"Oh, I didn't recognize you with your clothes on!" she laughed, peering at Matthew's face. "What's up? You look awful."

"Oh, ha ha. It could have had something to do with getting a fright seeing you!" he muttered.

"No, you do really," Sophie went on. "Your face is all pale and pinched. Perhaps you're coming down with something?"

"You don't look well, Matt. I said so this morning. Sophie's right. Are you sure you feel all right?" His mum looked concerned.

Matthew had had a bout of glandular fever the year before, which had knocked him for six. He'd had to miss a lot of school and he'd lost over a stone in weight. He'd put it all back on now. His mum was pleased that he was back to normal, so to see him looking off colour again worried her. She went on, "I told you when you got up that you looked poorly, but do you take any notice of me? I..."

"Mum!" interrupted Matthew, "I'm fine. I didn't sleep very well, that's all. I had this really weird dream about Wendles Wood. Dead lifelike and real."

"You should have heard him," nodded Russell in agreement, "moaning and groaning and wringing his hands. It was so funny!"

Matthew gave him a daggered look and Russell knew it was time to shut up.

"Well, are we going or not?" Matthew asked.

"Are you sure you feel well enough?" his mum repeated as Matthew nodded. "Anyway, where are you off to this morning?"

"We're going to visit my aunt in the village," said Sophie cheerily. The boys' eyes widened questioningly.

"I arranged it yesterday."

"Oh, well, that's all right, then," his mum nodded, her mind put at rest. "At least you'll be with a responsible adult if you start to feel ill!"

"She's obviously never met my aunt," whispered Sophie as they went out.

The three of them caught the local bus just

outside the campsite, into the village. It was only a ten minute ride, but Matthew said that he didn't feel like walking. In actual fact, he did feel a bit off colour. He wasn't sure if he was coming down with some bug or other, or if he was tired, or if the nightmare had caused it. It had certainly scared him, he knew that.

"We could have biked it, if your bike had been back," moaned Russell. "When did the repair shop say that it'd be ready?"

"The end of the week," Matthew answered shortly.

They got off the bus and walked down the green and gold leafy lane towards Sophie's aunt's house. Some leaves were just starting to fall from the trees, but some were very green still.

"This is it," announced Sophie proudly, leading them up a garden path to a quaint little cottage.

"This doesn't look like a medium's house!" quipped Russell. "I expected it to look something like the Munsters': all spiders and cobwebs, with a heavy brass knocker and things!"

Sophie laughed and Matthew clipped him lightly round the ear. Then Sophie knocked on the door and went in.

"Auntie Viv! It's me," she called, then turning to the boys she added, "come on in, she's expecting us."

"Of course she is, if she's a medium. There should have been no need for you to ring her in the first place," Russell joked.

They followed Sophie into the hallway and stood gaping at their surroundings. The hall was jam-packed with strange odds and ends, all clustered and cluttered together. There was a life-sized model of a gypsy standing in one corner. Large china butterflies were hung on the wall. A bullwhip thrown over a guitar, old wooden sewing machines, and a bookcase full of books and old records from the seventies. A large faded poster of some seventies pop group covered the wall over the top of coats piled onto a wooden chair.

"Wow!" said Russell. "Neat hallway!"

"Ey up, me dears. Get thy bums inside," came a voice from a room to the right. Matthew and Russell looked at one another with raised eyebrows.

"She's from Yorkshire," whispered Sophie.

"I see," smiled Matthew.

They walked into the lounge. The room was decorated in much the same fashion as the hallway. A record belted out from an old fashioned hi-fi in the corner. The boys recognised it as an old Eagles track that their parents sometimes played. The room was a hotchpotch of furniture and ornaments, but it had a style all of its own. Both of the boys straight away decided that they liked it. But no matter how the room impressed them, it paled into comparison with Auntie Viv! She was a big lady with long, wild hair. She had a lovely smiling face that made you feel instantly

42

welcome, and her eyes twinkled mischievously. She was very outrageous, they could tell that immediately. She was wearing a long, loose, multi-coloured blouse over black leggings and baseball pumps, which made her feet look too small to hold her up.

Sophie walked across to kiss her.

"Hello, Auntie. These are the friends I was telling you about, Matt and Russ. They're staying in our field."

Auntie Viv peered closely at them both with her twinkling eyes, then she smiled.

"Sooooo...these are the two bits of beef you were tellin' me about, our Soph. Not bad, eh? Thy was right, me ol' flower!"

Sophie went almost as red as Matthew and Russell.

"Auntie!" she hissed.

"Oh, I'm sorry, me an' my big gob! Now Soph tells me I can per'aps 'elp you in some way? So, me little 'taters, what's t'game, then?"

Matthew glanced across at the other two and they signalled for him to be the spokesperson. He told Auntie Viv the whole story, from his accident in Wendles Wood to his meetings with Ben, the last one being the day before. Auntie Viv listened carefully until he'd finished.

"Soph was right. It does sound like Ben Walker. Sophie, go an' put t'kettle on, flower, we'll 'ave a cuppa. Mattie, I need you to come an' sit by me."

Matthew hesitantly got up and moved across

the room to sit next to Auntie Viv.

"Oh, very nice, me ol' mate. Every colour thy could want," she exclaimed peering more closely at his damaged eye.

"Turn t'music down, Russ."

Russell went quickly across and did as he was told, after he'd worked out which knob to turn.

"Ben Walker, eh? Well there's a blast from t'past. I told them policemen 'e were dead. I just knew it, some'ow. None of 'em paid the slightest attention to me, though. So 'e's still in t'wood, is 'e. Poor lad. Some unresolved business, I'll be bound. Come 'ere, Mattie."

So saying she turned to Matthew and scooped up both of his hands in hers. Matthew was slightly embarrassed, but she held onto them firmly. She closed her eyes and turned her face to the ceiling. Her hands began to shake and she strained to control them. Matthew looked down at their joined hands, puzzled. Auntie Viv's face contorted suddenly. Then, with no warning at all, her hands flew away from Matthew's as though she'd had an electric shock.

Matthew and Russell were mesmerised. Matthew looked down at his hands again, turning them over. He felt a strange tingle in the tips of his fingers.

"By 'eck, Mattie, me lad," Auntie Viv finally said, gasping for breath and rubbing her hands together, as if she'd been stung. "Did thy know about that power?"

"Power?" asked Matthew, even more

puzzled. Russell looked at him in disbelief.

"Aye. Thy's got power, thy knows, if you'll use it an' let it out. More than me, if t'truth's known, but don't go blabbin' that about. I couldn't 'old you. You wouldn't let me in an' threw me off. Takes a right deal of strength, that."

Matthew stared at Auntie Viv in disbelief.

"I don't understand," he said, shaking his head.

"Nor me," Russell added.

"Well, you pair o' shop eggs, Mattie 'ere 'as powers, psychic powers. Stronger than any I've felt for a while. Did you say, you were t'only one t'see Ben?"

"Yes, so far. The others just missed him yesterday. He jogged away. I think he was scared that they wouldn't be able to see him," Matthew answered.

"I think Ben may be right. Don't count on anyone else bein' able to spot 'im. I'll bet you're the only one who can see 'im. You 'ave great ability, Mattie, me lad."

Matthew was shaking his head in disbelief.

"I know it must be difficult for you to take in, all at once, like, but I'm tellin' you, you 'ave psychic powers. You've seen a spirit. You'll probably find other strange things may start 'appenin', now your power is unlocked. I did."

"What kinds of things?" asked Russell.

"Oh, I don't know, per'aps..."

"Dreams?" interrupted Matthew, looking at his brother.

"Aye, could be one way the energy comes out. That 'appens to some of me mates, in our psychic circle."

They suddenly noticed Sophie at the door, holding a tray of tea. Her mouth was wide open in amazement.

"Come in, Soph and shut thy gob. You look like the Mersey Tunnel!" said her aunt.

"I can't believe what I've just heard," uttered Sophie.

"Well, believe it, Soph. Look, I'll prove it. Sit down an' all 'old 'ands."

Sophie sat next to Russell and the four of them joined hands.

"Concentrate, Mattie. Close your eyes and concentrate."

"What on?" he asked.

"Warmth, me ol' flower. Concentrate on warmth. Warm water, warm sun. Warmth."

Russell began to giggle, in spite of himself.

"Shut up, Russ!"

"Sorry," he apologised, trying to stifle his giggles.

They all sat around looking at Matthew.

"Concentrate, Mattie. That's it, good lad," Auntie Viv encouraged. Matthew had closed his eyes.

Without any warning at all, a red hot pain suddenly shot through Russell's hands.

"Ow!" he shouted and let go of the others' hands, fast. He'd leapt back and was surprised the others hadn't done the same. He rubbed his fingers.

"Wimp," said Sophie. "It wasn't that hot!"

Auntie Viv cackled. "Not for you Soph, but Russ is his brother. A bit too warm I think, Mattie, me ol' flower," was all she said.

"Will he be able to do this at home or school?" asked Russell, thinking of the endless lucrative possibilities for making money out of his brother.

"'E'd need a lot of practice, thy knows," answered Auntie Viv, "I 'elped to channel 'is energy a bit there."

They drank their tea and Matthew was unusually quiet. He kept looking down at his hands. All this was a bit too much to take in.

"So, what happens now?" asked Sophie.

"Well, me duck, Mattie 'ere 'olds the key. 'E can 'elp far more than me. Oh, crikey, I've started to talk in rhyme!" she cackled once more, then she added more seriously, "if I were you lot, I'd find out as much as I could about Ben's disappearance. I've always thought there was more to this business than first met the eye. The fact that Mattie's seen 'im means 'is spirit is some'ow stuck in that wood. Somethin' 'appened to 'im there. 'E can't rest or pass over fully till it's sorted. Mattie's right. Ben needs your 'elp."

"Will you help us, too?" Matthew asked Auntie Viv.

"If tha needs me, but I don't think tha will. You 'ave great power, me lad. More power than I've seen in one person, fer a while. Could be your age 'as somethin' to do wi' it."

"Age?" asked Sophie.

"Aye, Mattie's at that funny age. Fourteen. When I were a lass of fourteen I didn't know me bum from me elbow."

They all laughed. "Get thy bums down t'library round the corner. Look at the back copies of all the local newspapers. Ben's disappearance was very well covered. Find out all tha can, between you."

"What dates are we looking for?" Russell asked sensibly.

"Well, let's see, Russ. Ben Walker went missin'...it were around this time of the year, if I remember rightly. Um, it'd be three years ago. Our Sophie 'ad just 'ad 'er ninth birthday."

"That's what I told them." Sophie nodded.

"Clever clogs! Tha's not as daft as tha looks, our Soph." Auntie Viv smiled her twinkly smile, tickling her niece, until her legs kicked in the air and she screamed for mercy.

Chapter 8

The three of them sat crowded together in one small booth, at the local public library. Matthew had decided to strike while the iron was hot, and they had walked from Auntie Viv's house into the centre of the village, to the small library building.

Russell was turning the knob on the machine that contained all the back issues of local newspapers.

"I can't believe this isn't on computer disk, instead of this old thing," he grumbled. Pages of the local *Guardian* flashed in front of them. Every now and then Russell shot an enquiring glance at his brother.

"What's up with you, twirp face?" Matthew asked at last.

"You," answered his brother. "I always knew you were strange. Well, now I know for sure. My brother is a psycho!"

"Psychic, you fool," said Matthew.

"No, I was right the first time, I think," laughed Russell.

"There!" Sophie pointed suddenly, making them both jump. Russell whizzed the machine back a few pages. Sure enough, there it was, a front page article on Ben's disappearance. It was dated October 28th, 1992.

Matthew skimmed over the article and mumbled the main bits to the others.

"'Ben Walker, fourteen, disappeared from Home Farm campsite, Burden, two days ago.'"

"That would make it the 26th when he went missing," said Russell. Matthew and Sophie nodded.

"That's in two days," said Sophie. "Today's the 24th."

The boys looked at each other and a shiver ran up Matthew's spine. He carried on scanning the article.

"Er. 'No clues as to his disappearance. Police and members of the local community have taken up a search of Wendles Wood, where he was last seen by a couple from the village, Mr and Mrs Cowling.'"

"I know them!" said Sophie. "Mrs Cowling had a baby last year. Mum went out to deliver him. I bet Mum would know where they live."

"Jot that down," instructed Matthew, "we'll have a plan of action. We can talk to them, if we can find them."

Sophie nodded. Russell skimmed the words on the screen with his finger, carrying on from where Matthew left off.

"'Ben's damaged bicycle was found by police near Stile Copse at approximately 5pm on the evening of the 26th.' Stile Copse, isn't that where they found you?" Russell asked.

"Well, that's where Ben led me," answered Matthew.

"So you say," snapped Russell.

"What's your problem?" asked Matthew.

"I don't know," mumbled his brother, "I'm not sure about this stuff. Psychics, ghosties and Auntie Viv! Whoooo-oooo!" he laughed unconvincingly.

"You don't believe any of it, then?" asked Matthew.

"I want to. It's just that I'd like more proof."

"Please yourself," shrugged Matthew. "I know what I saw."

He knocked Russell's arm out of the way, none too gently, and finished off the article.

"'Ben's parents, Bill and Mary Walker, from Warrington, Cheshire, are said to be devastated, and are urging anyone who has any information relating to their son's disappearance to come forward. Police are still hopeful that Ben is alive, but a police spokesman commented that with every passing day hope fades a little more.'

We'll write to his parents, too." Matthew said quietly.

"We'll have to word it very carefully then," warned Sophie, "so as not to upset them. Mum is still in touch with them – Christmas cards and things. They're all still absolutely shattered."

"All?" Russell asked.

"Yes, Ben had a brother, John. Three years younger. He'd be fourteen, now. Same as you, Matt."

"Put that down on the list too, then, Sophie. We'll contact Ben's family. See if we can find out even more about the time of his disappearance.

Do you think your mum would do it, Sophie?"

"I don't see why not. What shall I tell her?" she asked.

"Say I might have found some new evidence. A clue as to why he disappeared." Russell shot him a look. "It's not lying," said Matthew. "I have found a clue, in a way. Oh, and ask if they can send a photo. That'll be the proof I need to show whether I really did see Ben or not..."

☠

Matthew sat bolt upright in bed. He glanced at his clock, its face glowing green in the darkness: 4.15 am. The sweat trickled down his back and his heartbeat pounded in his ears. He was frightened. He looked over to Russell, in the darkness. He was fast asleep with his mouth wide open. After a while, his eyes became accustomed to the darkness. He was amazed that he hadn't woken everyone up. He realised his shout had roused him from the middle of the dream. It was that same dream, only more real and more vivid. Especially the blood. He looked at his hands in the darkness, almost afraid of what he would see. Were they covered in blood? Was the blood dripping from them? He couldn't see anything really, just the outline of his fingers. All the same he decided he wouldn't put the light on to check. Just in case.

Chapter 9

Matthew and Russell called for Sophie early the next morning. Matthew was eager to go into the village to talk to the Cowlings, the couple who had last seen Ben in the wood. Sophie was surprised to see them so early and stumbled out of her front door, still trying to pull on her coat. She was wrestling with one of her sleeves which was inside out, much to Russell's amusement.

"Hello, you two," she mumbled, a piece of toast between her teeth. "You're early."

"Did you get the Cowlings' address?" asked Matthew, none too politely.

"Good morning, Sophie, sleep well did you? Lovely to see you this bright and breezy day!" Sophie said sarcastically. Russell giggled. He liked to see his brother taken down a peg or two occasionally.

"Sorry, Soph," Matthew apologised. "Well, did you?"

Sophie poked out her tongue at him, then with a flourish fished out a piece of paper from her coat pocket.

"Mum's fairly certain that they're still at this address: 14 Birch Avenue."

"Do you know whereabouts it is?" asked Russell.

"I had a look on my dad's map. It's this side of the village, should only take us about twenty minutes to walk," answered Sophie.

"You're not bad for a girl," smiled Russell.

"Can we catch the bus?" grumbled Matthew.

"It's not worth it, lazybones!" said Sophie, then looked concerned. "You're not still feeling a bit yuk, are you?"

"He's always very yuk!" interrupted Russell. Matthew raised his eyes to the heavens.

"No, I'm fine. Come on," he answered shortly, striding away. Sophie gave Russell a dirty look.

"What?" he said, jogging after them.

Sophie was almost spot on with her estimation and they reached the Cowlings' about twenty minutes later. Sophie marched up the path first, with the boys trailing behind her, and she rang the bell. Mrs Cowling answered the door, with a wriggling baby on her hip.

"Hello, Sophie," she said brightly. "What brings you here? So early, too! Is your mum okay?"

"Fine, thanks," nodded Sophie. "Mrs Cowling, we were wondering if you could help us clear something up. Matthew, my friend here, had a fall in the wood a few days ago."

"Ouch! Yes, so I see," she smiled, as she disentangled the baby's chubby fingers from her hair.

"Well, he thinks he may have found a clue to Ben Walker's disappearance. Do you remember Ben?" asked Sophie.

"Of course I do, I'm not likely to forget him,

am I? I think Roger and I were the last people to see him, the day he disappeared in Wendles Wood," she said thoughtfully.

She suddenly leaned out of her doorway and looked up and down the avenue, quite furtively, Matthew thought.

"Come in a minute, let me put my squirmy, wriggly son down."

They walked into the lounge and sat on the sofa. Mrs Cowling put her son on the floor amongst a mountain of toys and he gurgled with delight.

"How old is he?" asked Russell.

"Fourteen months," smiled Mrs Cowling. Russell slid off the sofa and lay alongside the baby. He began to build towers of bricks which the baby took delight in knocking over. "Mind your hair, he loves tugging at it. Oops, too late!" warned Mrs Cowling.

The baby was chuckling with delight. Both of his hands were intertwined with Russell's curly hair. He was bouncing Russell's head up and down on the carpet, like a ball. Russell eased the baby's grip a little and laughed.

"It's okay, honest!" he giggled.

Matthew and Sophie were laughing too, both secretly impressed at the ease with which Russell played with the toddler.

"About the same mental age, you see," said Matthew, and Russell pretended that he hadn't heard.

"So, how can I help you?" Mrs Cowling asked.

"We need to know if you can remember when and where you saw Ben on that day," said Matthew. "We're trying to piece it all together, you see."

"Well, I can only tell you what I told the police at the time."

"That's fine, Mrs Cowling," said Sophie.

"What is it exactly that you've discovered?" Mrs Cowling asked Matthew. Matthew faltered for a minute, before saying, "I'm not sure, but I think I may have found one of Ben's handkerchiefs. His initials were in one of the corners."

"I see," said Mrs Cowling thoughtfully. "I think it's very unlikely, though, after all this time. Don't you? The handkerchief could belong to anyone. All things considered it may be as well to leave things alone. No point in dragging this back up again after all this time. You'll upset his family dreadfully. Whatever happened on 26th October three years ago, no one will ever know."

"Can we just ask you where you saw Ben?" Russell asked gently, sensing that Mrs Cowling was becoming upset.

"Well, Roger and I had gone for a walk. It was a couple of months after we'd been married. Anyway, we were walking by the stream, near to the clearing where they chopped down all of those oak trees about five years ago. We saw Ben there. He was sitting on one of the tree stumps, looking very grumpy, if

I remember. He said hello though. Seemed a nice enough lad."

"What was he wearing?" asked Matthew suddenly.

"Oh, lord. I can't remember. Just ordinary clothes. Jeans, I think. Why?"

"Just wondered. Had he got a bike?"

"Yes, as a matter of fact, he had. It was leaning up against one of the tree stumps."

"What time was it, can you remember?" Russell asked, sitting up.

"It was late afternoon. I'd say about four o'clock. Just about to get dark. That's about it, I'm afraid." Matthew looked at her, thoughtfully. There was more to this than met the eye. He was sure of it.

Russell tickled the baby and then jumped up from the floor.

"Thank you ever so much, Mrs Cowling," said Sophie smiling. The boys mumbled their thanks, too. Matthew though looked very sullen. Not like him at all.

Mrs Cowling showed them to the door.

"You haven't told the police about that handkerchief, have you?" she asked them.

"Not yet, but we're going to," replied Matthew. "We just wanted to clear a few things up first. Make sure it was Ben's hanky, for a start!"

"I really wouldn't bother. It's pretty unlikely that a handkerchief could stay preserved for three years. It would have rotted. You don't want to reopen this case on a red herring like that. I think you'd be wasting their time. It was nice to see you though, Sophie." The baby had followed her to the door. She scooped him up into her arms and plonked him on her hip. Then she opened the door and saw them out.

As they turned back to wave, Matthew noticed that she was looking up and down the avenue again, almost as if she was checking that no one had seen them coming and going.

"Interesting," Russell said.

"There's something she's not telling us," Matthew said.

"She may have just been upset," said Sophie.

"But she didn't really tell us anything," Matthew went on.

"Yes, she did," Russell said thoughtfully. "They saw Ben at four o'clock. That newspaper we read said Matthew's bike had been found by police that same evening. Seems strange, don't you think, such a short time."

"You're right!" said Sophie. "She said they'd seen Ben in Oak Tree Clearing, by the stream. I know where that is and it's a good hour's walk from Stile Copse, where they found the bike."

"But it wouldn't have taken that long on a bike, little Miss Clever," said Matthew.

"No, maybe not. Except the paths from that clearing are overgrown. It's impossible to ride down them. You have to get off and push. You'd hit a tree root or rip your legs to pieces, trying to ride. No, he must have pushed it. But Russ is right, the time thing is strange. Hardly enough

58

time for him to get to Stile Copse on his bike. Perhaps she got the time wrong, eh?"

"Or perhaps Ben didn't take his bike to Stile Copse. What if something happened to him, say he was shot or something and someone else took it there to cover their tracks," Matthew reasoned.

"Bit melodramatic!" quipped Russell.

"Oh shut up," Matthew snapped.

They walked along in silence for a while.

"What time is it?" Matthew asked at last.

"Half past ten," answered Russell.

"Have we got time to go to Oak Tree Clearing? I'd like to see it. I've got the weirdest feeling I know it, somehow," said Matthew.

"Follow me!" shouted Sophie, jogging away from them.

"Come on, I know a short cut over this field. Just keep your eye out for the bulls."

"Bulls! Forget it!" Russell stopped dead in his tracks.

"Only joking, idiot!" laughed Sophie. Russell ran fast to catch up with her, but as always she outran him at every turn.

Chapter 10

"Are we nearly there?" moaned Russell. "It's lunch at one o'clock. Will we be home in time?"

"It's only quarter past eleven, we've got loads of time. Look, we're here now, anyway." Sophie pointed ahead of her.

The children stepped suddenly from the cool, silent darkness of the wood into a small bright clearing. Shafts of sunlight shone down on the green grass and on the tree stumps.

"That's where they cut down some of the oak trees," Sophie pointed again. "Matt?"

Matthew was standing in the middle of the clearing, looking around frantically at the paths leading from it. The clearing was familiar, very familiar.

"I knew I recognised your description of this place. This is where I stopped to rest, that day just before my accident. I fell asleep just here." He walked up to a tree stump and pointed. "You were right, too. I did try and ride my bike along one of the paths. Something spooked me. That's when I hit a tree root and fell off."

Russell and Sophie looked on as Matthew got more and more excited. Then he suddenly stopped and seemed to be staring into the wood, at one tree in particular.

"What's up with him, now?" asked Russell. They both jumped as Matthew suddenly shouted out one word, "Ben!"

They looked at each other as Matthew ran to the tree just out of the sunlight.

"Wait there!" he turned and called to them both.

"Glad to," mumbled Russell. "Can you see anyone, Soph?" he asked her.

"Nope," she answered.

"He's lost it," Russell said, shaking his head.

Matthew ran just into the wood, where Ben was standing, watching them.

"Hi!" he shouted. "Come on, I'll introduce you to my brother."

"Hello, Matt," Ben answered, shaking his head at the same time. "It's no use, they won't be able to see me. Sophie hasn't seen me once yet. I've seen her every time she's come into the wood. She's growing up before my very eyes and I'm stuck here," he said sadly. "What's your brother's name?"

"Russ. It's Russ." Matthew answered.

Ben walked a little way into the clearing and waved his arms.

"Russ! Sophie! Over here!" he shouted loudly. Matthew watched their faces. There was no reaction from them. Nothing.

"Russ!" Matthew called. Russell looked up straight away to see what his brother wanted. He was looking straight through Ben.

"You okay?" Russell called.

"Yes, it's nothing. I'll be there in a minute," Matthew answered and watched as Ben walked back to him.

"Told you," Ben shrugged.

"We want to help you," said Matthew.

"How? It's useless," answered Ben.

"Sophie's aunt says you're stuck here because of some 'unresolved business'. Do you know what that could be?"

"No," answered Ben. "It took me ages to work out I was dead! I can't remember any of it. I remember sitting in that clearing and saying hello to a couple. I must've looked pretty grumpy, I was in a right mood after that argument with my parents. Then I pushed my bike along one of the paths and that's it. The next thing I know I'm dead!"

Matthew smiled and Ben looked hurt.

"Sorry," he apologised. "It's just that you described it as though it happens to everyone. I can't even begin to imagine how you feel. But listen, I've been having some pretty weird dreams about this place and about two men with guns."

Ben froze immediately.

"What?" he whispered.

"Two men with guns," Matthew repeated. Ben was frowning as if trying to remember something.

"Guns? Yes, I do remember very vaguely. Birds and guns, but how does that fit in?"

"I'm not sure yet. But we're going to work it out between us. We're going to help you, Ben."

"Thanks," said Ben as he began jogging away into the trees. "I believe you will. Well, you have already. I need to check something out. See you."

"Where are you going? Wait!" called Matthew, but it was too late and Ben was out of sight. He knew that Ben hadn't got anything to 'check out' at all and walked back over to the others.

"What have you been doing over by that tree, mumbling to yourself like an idiot?" asked Russell.

"It was Ben. I was talking to Ben," Matthew said simply.

"Well, we didn't see him," said Russell.

"I know," answered Matthew.

"Auntie Viv said we may not be able to, so shut up Russ," snapped Sophie.

"Ohhh, shut up, Russ," mimicked Russell in a ridiculously high voice.

"Let's go," said Matthew.

As they stood up, Sophie pointed to the path they had to take, then stopped dead.

Two men had appeared before them in the clearing. None of them were sure where they had come from, or how long they had been there. The men stood side by side with their legs apart and their hands thrust into heavy overcoats. They had hoods covering their heads and more sinister still, it was impossible to see their faces.

Matthew felt a shiver run up his spine. There was something all too familiar about these men. He ushered Russell and Sophie behind him, not knowing why. They stood facing the men. Matthew knew that trying to outrun them would be a last resort. No one spoke for a while. At last it was Matthew who broke the silence.

"What do you want?" he called. They didn't answer for what seemed like an age, until one of them said, "We know where you are. Wherever you go, we're watching you."

"I don't like this," whispered Sophie, "they're scaring me."

"Who are you?" called Russell.

"None of your business," one of them shouted back. "Just remember that we know you."

Then they laughed together. Horrible, hollow laughs that made Matthew sick with fear. He'd heard those laughs before. He recognized the men now, just as he recognized the laughter. They were the men in his dream. They were real! He pulled Russell and Sophie closer in behind him.

"Owww!" protested Russell. "What do you think you're doing?"

"We know you've been poking your nose into things that don't concern you," the men shouted.

"We don't know what you mean," Matthew called.

"The library, the Cowlings, that weird medium woman, Ben Walker. If you know what's good for you, lay off. You've no idea of what you're getting yourselves tied up in. Keep your noses out!"

"It's dangerous," the other one spoke now. "You never know what might happen to little children who mess with danger. You might get yourselves hurt. Killed even!"

They laughed again. Loud laughs that rang out

64

around the clearing. Then one of them moved his overcoat slightly and a glint of sunlight flashed on something metallic underneath.

Matthew acted quickly, sensing the danger they were in.

"They've got guns!" he hissed. "When I give the word, we'll run for it. It's our only chance...NOW!"

He pulled Russell and Sophie frantically behind him and they ran down the nearest pathway, the one Ben had disappeared down earlier. Matthew looked back and to his horror saw the men start after them. The guns were clearly visible now. The men were running with them in their hands.

"Run!" he called. "Sophie, which way is it?" Sophie was scared. Matthew could see her face - a picture of terror.

"Take the left fork at the bottom of this dip," she called out breathlessly. Russell tripped and stumbled. Matthew pulled him to his feet. They looked at each other and an expression of fright crossed Russell's face. He pulled free of Matthew's grip and ran on even faster.

"Run!" Matthew called, "run, Russ!"

Russell had begun to cry as he was running and the tears rolled silently down his cheeks.

Matthew looked back. The men were still coming.

"At the fork in the pathway, go left. In the dip, by the side of the path you'll be safe. Stay there and hide. They won't look there," a calm voice said in Matthew's ear. Matthew didn't question it. He did as he was told. He pulled Sophie after him. Russell scampered the same way. Matthew threw himself into the dip by the side of the path and hit the floor. The other two did the same. Matthew motioned for them to keep quiet. They needed no second telling. Russell kept his head down, almost afraid to look at his brother.

Matthew listened out for the men. As he did so a strong, familiar, peaty smell filled his nostrils. He frowned, trying to remember where he had smelt it before. Perhaps it was when he had fallen and cut his head. He wasn't sure.

Russell wiped his eyes so that the others couldn't see, but left dirty smears all over his face. The men came closer, still running, guns held at hip level. The three of them could clearly see them.

"You know where we are?" they heard one say, and then, "Let's get out of here. We've scared them off."

They ran on, past the dip by the side of the pathway, and were soon out of sight.

"They've gone!" said Sophie with a sigh of relief.

"Yes," Matthew got up carefully. "How did you know about this hideaway?" he asked her.

"I didn't," she answered. They both looked at Russell.

"I didn't either," said Russell quietly. Matthew smiled.

66

"It looks like Ben saved the day again." Then he noticed Russell's face and asked, "What's up? Were you scared of them?"

"Not the men," Russell answered. "Well, I mean I was frightened of them, but I was more scared of you, Matthew."

"What are you on about?" his brother frowned. "I'm sorry if I pulled you a bit too hard, but..."

"It's not that," Russell mumbled. "What colour are your eyes?"

"That's a daft question. You know they're brown."

"Well, when I tripped up and you pulled me up, I looked at your face. Your eyes weren't brown, Matthew. They were blue, a deep blue..."

Chapter 11

"I still don't see why we can't tell the police," moaned Russell. "Those men chased us and threatened us. We have to tell someone. I'm telling Mum and Dad, at least."

"No, you're not! Not yet," said Matthew. "We will eventually, but not yet. We need more proof."

"What proof? You want to wait until they actually shoot us?"

"Listen," said Matthew, "I think those two men had something to do with Ben's death."

"Why?" said Russell in disbelief.

"I think they may have even killed him."

"Don't be daft," said Russell again, his eyes widening as he became frightened.

"They're the same men that I dreamed about. You know, those weird dreams I've been having. It's them!"

"How do you know, though?" asked Russell.

"I just have this feeling, that's all. Think about it. Why else would they want to warn us off? We're getting too close, that's why."

"Yes, I suppose that makes sense," shrugged Russell. He hesitated for a moment then added, "How come your eyes changed colour, then, when we were running away from them?"

"I've no idea. I didn't even know that they had," Matthew said truthfully. "I really didn't mean to scare you, Russ."

"I know, but it did," said Russell quietly. "I still think we should tell Mum and Dad."

"Soon," promised Matthew.

"What if those men come after us again? We could be hurt."

"What if I punch you smack on the nose?" answered Matthew.

"Try it!" Russell jumped to his feet and started jigging about on his toes, already in a defensive shotokan karate stance. Matthew took him up and for five minutes they sparred around the lounge of the caravan, adding their own, very loud sound effects.

"We could've taken those men on, Matt!" boasted Russell.

"Don't be daft. They had guns! They were men, too. Remember what Dave says at karate – don't try and fight an adult. If you can, run! If not, hurt them and then run! There was no point in trying to fight them, we could have been shot!"

"What on earth is going on?" Their mum and dad had come in from the kitchen.

"Stop it, you two!" ordered their dad. "Russ, you know Matt has a bad eye, don't hit your brother like that!"

The brothers stopped and then their dad added, "hit him like this!"

Then their dad was in the fray and all three of them were fighting and rolling about in a heap on the lounge floor.

"I give up!" shrugged their mum. "I'm

surrounded by madmen. I'm going to make a cup of tea."

As she walked out, a cushion flew through the air and hit her smack on the back of the head.

A loud knock on the door interrupted the wrestling match. Russell disentangled himself from the heap and went to answer it.

"Oh, hello, Soph," he said, red-faced and breathless.

"Come in."

"I've been knocking for ages," she said. "You pair have been making a right row! Your mum and dad would kill you. Where are they?"

She followed Russell into the lounge, where Matthew and his dad were picking themselves up from the floor and dusting themselves off. They were still tip-tapping at each other and giggling. Sophie's mouth opened. She was slightly shocked, but smiled hello.

Matthew and Russell put on their jackets and trainers and left with Sophie.

"See you later!" they called to their parents.

The three of them walked to the den just inside the wood.

"Your dad seems nice. Almost as mad as you two!" said Sophie smiling. "My dad wouldn't dream of rolling around on the floor with me!"

"Yep, our parents are okay," said Matthew, which was high praise indeed. Then on a more serious note he added, "We'll stay in the den today. I don't want us to go any further into the

70

wood. Just in case those men might be about."

"You haven't said anything about yesterday, have you, Soph?" asked Russell.

"No, but I wanted to. They really frightened me. I think we should tell someone, soon," she replied.

"We will. Just let's wait a bit, eh. We need more proof. More to tell them, so that they'll believe us," answered Matthew.

"You know today's the 26th," said Sophie solemnly. "It's the anniversary of Ben's death."

They all looked at each other.

"So? I don't think that's going to change anything," said Russell.

"It might!" said Sophie dramatically. "Oh, by the way, I nearly forgot. My mum telephoned Ben's parents. They sent a letter back. It came this morning, just general news about how they are and the holidays they've been on. Er, they also sent this." She pulled a photograph from her pocket and handed it first to Russell. "It was taken the day before Ben disappeared."

Russell looked at the photograph, then turned it over.

"Ben, October 25th 1992, in his favourite gear."

Matthew hung back, wanting to snatch the photograph from Russell, but afraid to.

"Here, Matt, you have to look some time."

Matthew took the photograph and looked at it for a long time. The others watched him. Then he smiled. A blonde haired young man smiled back at him. He was wearing jeans and a black T-shirt and he had deep blue eyes.

"It's him," he said simply.

Chapter 12

"At the fork, go to the left, in the dip."

The voice jolted Matthew out of a deep sleep. He sat up too quickly, then lay back down again. He felt awful, his head ached all over, and his throat felt raw. One minute he was red hot and sweating buckets, and the next his teeth were chattering because he was so cold. It had started just after lunch and his mum had sent him straight to bed with two aspirin. She knew he wasn't well when he didn't argue.

He'd slept for a little while and expected to feel better when he woke up. But he didn't. He was getting worse. While he was asleep, he kept hearing that same voice in his head.

"At the fork, go to the left, in the dip."

It was a whisper at first, but it kept getting louder and louder. Matthew knew it must have been Ben's voice, but it didn't sound like Ben. It was all so mixed up. The men, the ghost of a boy who had died three years ago today, the wood, his accident. It hurt his head to think of it all. The whole lot was whizzing round and round and he'd given up trying to make sense of it but it just wouldn't go away.

He pulled his quilt up to his chin and sighed. He felt so ill it was untrue.

Soon, though, he'd drifted off to sleep once more. His mum popped in to check on him about ten minutes later. Matthew was still asleep, but was mumbling and wringing the quilt with his hands. He was soaked with sweat and was red-faced and flushed. She felt her son's forehead. It was burning hot. She shook him gently to wake him, but he carried on mumbling. The cut above his eye seemed to stand out even more than usual. It looked very red and sore.

"Russ!" she shouted. Russell ran in. "Get your dad to go to the farmhouse and ask Mary to ring for a doctor. I can't wake your brother and he's really feverish. Bring me a flannel and a bowl of cold water. I must try and get his temperature down."

Russell dashed out and a few seconds later his dad came in.

"He's frightening me, John," she said to her husband. "I can't wake him up."

"Matt?" his dad called, shaking him gently, "Matt, come on son!"

But Matthew wasn't there. He was in the wood, at Oak Tree Clearing. He was sitting on one of the tree stumps looking very angry, tearing at the grass and throwing it towards the trees as hard as he could. It just wasn't fair. His parents never let him do anything he wanted. They just didn't understand. They never listened to his side of things. He only wanted to go into town with some friends. Where was the harm in that?

Russell suddenly appeared from the trees and stood in front of him.

"Well, that's how your eyes changed colour," he said.

"What?"

"Your eyes were brown and now they're blue. First you were Matthew and now you're Ben," he said seriously and then walked away, back into the darkness of the wood.

Matthew stopped in mid-dream to take stock of the situation, the way you can sometimes, in dreams. He looked down at himself. He was wearing jeans, a black T-shirt and trainers that weren't his. He recognised them, but they were Ben's, not his. There was a bike leaning against one of the tree stumps. The bike wasn't his either. It was a nice one, but it wasn't his. He suddenly realised he wasn't himself, somehow. Well, he was, but there was someone else, too.

Two people suddenly crossed through the clearing. The couple cut in front of him.

"Hello," they mouthed. He couldn't actually hear the words. It was as if someone had turned down the volume control. Everything was silent. He said hello back and recognised the woman. It was Mrs Cowling, who they had met a few days before, or was it yesterday, or even this morning? He couldn't remember. He looked at his watch, ten past four. He thought about going back. It would be dark, soon. But he decided against it. He'd let them stew for a bit longer. Scare them and let them think he'd gone for good.

He picked up the bike, that he knew wasn't really his, and began to push it down one of the paths. It would have been impossible to ride, it was so overgrown. He'd been walking for a while when he heard a sharp crack overhead. He looked up to see a large brown bird falling towards him. It fell in slow motion, catching on twigs and branches on the way down. It landed at his feet. Its plumage was beautiful. So many colours all intermingled together.

Just like my eye, he thought and gingerly touched his cut. But there was nothing there. The gash above his eye had gone.

He bent down to look at the bird and he stroked its soft body. It was still warm. Then he noticed that it had been shot. It was dead. He looked back down the path and could just make out someone coming towards him. He pushed his bike behind a bush and crouched down. He didn't know why. He wanted to see whoever it was, but for some reason he didn't want them to see him.

A boy of about sixteen walked up the path towards the bird. He picked it up by its feet and carried it back the way he had just come. It swung heavily at his side, its head and neck, loose and limp. Matthew was angry. He got up and pushed his bike back down the path, following the boy. How dare he shoot birds like that.

As he was walking he heard other shots, the only sounds he could hear. He began to run towards the noise, unafraid. Suddenly he burst out into the clearing. Oak Tree Clearing. He dropped his bike and tried to shout, No! but no sound came out.

There were two of them sitting on tree stumps, with dead birds laid out all around them. Matthew couldn't see their faces properly, but he knew they were laughing. He could see their shoulders moving up and down. They were laughing at him.

It was misty in the clearing. The mist closed in and hung heavily on the branches of the trees. Matthew stood defiantly looking at the figures of the two boys. One of them picked up his gun. He was mouthing words, but Matthew couldn't tell what they were. Then, they were laughing again.

Matthew ran at them in blind anger. To his horror, he saw the one with the gun pull it up to shoulder level. He mouthed something at Matthew, then Matthew heard a sound. It splintered the silence of the wood. It was a sudden crack. It reverberated round the trees, echoing. It was the sound of a gun shot.

The force of the shot hitting him knocked him back onto the floor, but he fell in slow motion.

He became aware of an enormous pain in his side. He looked down at it, holding himself where it hurt. He was bleeding. He lifted his hands and looked at them closely. They were covered in blood.

The boys were standing stock still, just watching him. They seemed shocked, frightened even.

"Help me!" he mouthed.

One of them turned, picked up some of the birds, threw them into the wood in all directions, then ran. The other followed close behind. They had been afraid, he was sure of it.

Matthew lay on his back on the ground. He lifted up his T-shirt and looked down. He was surprised that the wound wasn't that serious. It was bleeding a lot, though, and he felt it carefully. From what he could tell, it was what they called a 'flesh wound' in the old cowboy movies. The shot had glanced his side. It was just a surface wound, but it was bleeding. He knew he had to apply pressure to stop it. He placed both hands on his side and pressed down hard. With a great effort he turned himself over and pushed himself up. He stumbled along the nearest pathway to get out of the wood and to get help. He looked down again at his hands. Blood was seeping through his fingers and dripping onto his jeans. He could see that happening, even in the half-light.

He half ran, half stumbled and suddenly heard the words, "At the fork to the left, in the dip," ringing around his head. He came to the fork in the path and took the left one, as he'd been told. He was running too fast for his legs to keep up with him and his foot caught on a tree root or something sticking up out of the ground. He tripped and fell, banging his head too hard on a stone. The blackness swam

78

around his head. The ground smelled earthy and rich. A strong, peaty smell. Too sick to move any further, he breathed in the comforting earth and at that moment, Ben's persona engulfed him. He sobbed and then passed out.

Matthew struggled. It was a close thing. He struggled away from Ben before he, too, was swallowed into the blackness. He was fighting, lashing out and fighting for his very life. Then, suddenly, it was over. He felt soothing hands on his forehead.

A coolness to quench the fire, dampen the heat, and he drifted back peacefully to the wood, through what seemed like an endless black tunnel. He heard the sound of spades on earth, was aware of the grass, pine, and peaty smells of the wood. Through a misty darkness, and by torchlight, he saw the outline of two figures digging. Their shovels clanked on stones. He watched them, puzzled.

"To the left, in the dip," came into his mind.

Then he was back. It was daylight once more. He was crouching down in the dip, the place where he'd just seen the two figures digging. He was crouching right upon that place, waiting for someone. Someone was coming, jogging past him.

It was a boy, about the same age as him. He was wearing jeans and a black T-shirt. He had blonde hair and deep blue eyes.

"Ben!" Matthew said, surprised. He stood up.

"Hello, Matt," said Ben, smiling. He put out his hand to help Matthew out of the dip by the side of the path.

"Let me help you out of there," Ben said, "the way you're going to help me."

The two boys held each other's forearm and suddenly Matthew understood it all.

"You were shot," said Matthew. Ben nodded.

"So it seems."

"I don't think that was what killed you, though. It was the fall that did it, I'm pretty sure. You hit a stone or something just as hard," Matthew explained.

"Yes, I felt it. I couldn't remember before, I wouldn't have remembered without your help," Ben said.

"It's okay," said Matthew.

"I'll be going soon," Ben announced.

"Going? Where?"

"I'll be able to move on, soon. We did it together."

"Why? I don't understand?" Matthew frowned.

"I think you do Matt," Ben smiled. "You know where I am now."

"Yes," answered Matthew.

"Tell them, Matt. Tell them where I am. Tell them I'm here."

Chapter 13

"Ben's in the wood. Wendles Wood. At the fork in the path, go left and jump in the dip," Matthew mumbled.

"A little way off the clearing, there in the dip, where we hid from the men. The smell, peaty, earthy smells. Ben's there!" he shouted and sat bolt upright in bed.

His family came running in, to see what all the noise was about.

"Matt?" said his mum, sitting on the edge of his bed feeling his forehead. "Matt, are you okay?"

He lay back down.

"I'm fine, now, I feel a lot better," he said.

"We've been worried about you," his dad said looking concerned and sitting on the other side of Matthew's bed.

"You've been quite ill all afternoon and evening. You had a right temperature!"

"You punched Dad right on the ear!" smiled Russell, relieved to see his brother awake, even though he would never have admitted it. "You were rolling about, lashing out with your arms and legs, and all the time you were fast asleep. Your eyes were closed. It was brill!"

"Russell, don't talk daft. Do you want a drink, Matt?" asked his mum.

"Yes, please. I'm really thirsty."

"Get him a drink Russ, will you. You seem a

lot cooler now. The doctor said if you got any worse, or your temperature got any higher, you'd have had to go into hospital," his mum said, frowning concern.

"Doctor?" said Matthew puzzled.

"Yes, a doctor came. Mum was dabbing you down with ice cold water. You were in the nuddy," Russell giggled.

"So?" shrugged Matthew.

"It was a woman!" Russell giggled again, as Matthew pulled the quilt over his head, groaning.

"The doctor told me I was doing the right thing, getting your temperature down," his mum said laughing. "No doubt she's seen it all before, people's bits and pieces."

"Well, she hadn't seen my bits and pieces before!" Matthew said with embarrassment, taking his drink from Russell.

"She said you had a viral infection, Matt," Russell told him. "I said that you were a viral infection on legs," he added, giggling.

"Well, I feel much better, now. In fact I'm starving," Matthew announced.

"We saved you some tea. I'll fetch it," his dad said.

"I'll help," said his mum. "I'll get you some clean bedclothes as well. These are soaking. Third lot, too," she mumbled, wondering how on earth she was going to get all of it washed.

"Sorry, Mum," Matthew apologised as his mum left. She smiled and kissed him on his forehead and he didn't try to stop her.

82

Russell got up to follow his parents out, but Matthew grabbed his arm and pulled him back.

"Wait, Russ!" he hissed. They both waited until their parents were out of earshot. "Russ, I know where Ben is!"

Russell looked puzzled.

"What are you talking about?" he asked.

"I know how and when he died and I know where his body is."

Russell shook his head in disbelief. "How?"

"While I was ill, I had this really vivid dream. It wasn't like a normal dream at all. I was there. I was Ben. I had Ben's eyes, Russ. They were blue, like they were that time we were running away from the men. I saw the Cowlings. I saw the two men who tried to scare us off, only they were youths, then. One of them shot me, well Ben. Well, you know."

"Shot him? So that's how he died?" Russell was trying hard to piece all Matthew's ramblings together.

"No, that isn't what killed him," Matthew explained, "it was only a surface wound. Bled a lot, though. Ben fell and hit his head, just like I did. Only he never came round. The fall killed him. I think the two men who shot him, found him, got scared and hid him. They buried his body, so they wouldn't get caught."

"Crikey!" said Russell. "Now, can we tell Mum and Dad?"

"I think we'd better," Matthew answered. "Then we'll have to go to the police."

After Matthew had eaten he announced that he felt well enough to get up. He knew there was a lot to do. The family sat in the lounge watching the television.

"Dad?" Matthew began, "do you remember after my fall, when you and the policeman found me?"

"Yes," his dad answered, only half listening.

"Do you remember that I said a boy had led me out of the wood to safety. Ben. Ben Walker? Well I wasn't imagining it. He did find me and lead me out. The only thing is, Dad, Ben Walker died in Wendles Wood three years ago today."

His dad turned to face him. He had switched off the television and was listening intently. His mum was looking at him with a worried expression. Russell glanced around at them all, trying to weigh up the situation.

"Are you still feeling poorly? How's your temperature?" his mum asked him, feeling his forehead with her hand, once again.

"I'm fine. Sophie knew about Ben Walker, didn't she, Russ." Russell nodded. Matthew gabbled on. "His family used to come here on holiday, like us. He disappeared three years ago. I know, though, that he died in the wood. We found his handkerchief. I think I know where he is, too. I've been having some weird dreams. There were these two men, as well..."

"Matthew," soothed his mum, "Matt, you haven't been well. You've had a very high

84

temperature. It may have made you see things that weren't really there."

"I see Ben as clearly as I see you and Dad," explained Matthew, "don't I Russ?"

Everyone turned to look at Russell. He nodded again.

"Russ was with you, when you saw this boy called Ben?"

"Yes, and Sophie," said Matthew, looking at Russell for support.

"Did you or Sophie see this lad called Ben?" asked his mum.

"Well, no. Not really, but Auntie Viv said that..." answered Russell.

"Auntie Viv?" questioned his dad.

"Back to bed with you, Matt!" said his mum. "Get some rest, now. Things will look a lot better in the morning. Don't worry about these dreams. They're perfectly natural and common with such a high temperature. Off you go, love."

Matthew glowered at Russell as he walked out of the lounge and back to bed. Russell shrugged apologetically.

"Plan B, then," muttered Matthew, before he drifted off into one of the most deep and restful sleeps he'd had for a long time.

Chapter 14

When he woke up the next morning, Matthew was back to his usual self. He ate a big breakfast, to the beaming smiles of his parents. None of them uttered a word about the conversation they'd had the night before.

"You look a lot better, Matt," Russell said, a bit ashamed that he hadn't done more to back his brother up the evening before.

"I feel a lot better," Matthew replied. "Is it okay if me and Russ call for Sophie this morning and go to visit her aunt on the bus?" he asked his mum. Russell looked surprised at his request.

"I'm not sure if you're up to it, Matt. Do you feel all right?" she said.

"I feel fine, now. I need some fresh air," he smiled.

"All right. But be careful!" she warned.

The brothers got ready quickly, before their mum changed her mind, and were soon walking towards the farmhouse on the campsite.

"Sorry about last night, Matt. I could've backed you up a bit more," Russell said.

"That's all right. There's nothing you could have done. There was no way they were going to believe us, was there?"

Russell shook his head. They knocked on the farmhouse door and Sophie answered, looking surprised to see them.

"Are you okay?" she asked Matthew. "When I called for you yesterday afternoon, you were on your deathbed."

"You're not far wrong there," smiled Matthew. "I thought we'd go to see your Auntie Viv. Is that all right?"

"What's happened?" Sophie looked puzzled. "I should think that would be okay. I'll just ring her to make sure. Why, though?"

"We'll tell you on the way," said Matthew. "Just ring your Auntie Viv and tell her that we're coming."

Sophie ran back inside and appeared a few minutes later, pulling on her trainers.

"Come on, then. I'm ready, Auntie Viv says she's put the kettle on. Now tell me, what's all this about, what's going on?"

They caught the bus to Auntie Viv's. Matthew didn't quite feel up to walking. They talked all the way and were there within thirty minutes. Sophie had become very quiet, trying to take in everything that Matthew had told her.

They walked up the path and knocked on the door. They heard her call for them to come in.

"Door's open!" she yelled. As they entered, she met them in the hall, carrying a tray of tea. She looked as weird and wonderful as ever. She was wearing a loose flowery top and red leggings, with enormous banana feet slippers. Her hair sprang out all over the place.

"Come through 'ere, me little cherubs! 'Ey up, 'ow are you all? Look at Russell's little face, couldn't you just eat 'im up!" she said.

"Do you remember when you said we could ask you for help, if we needed it?" Matthew asked and Auntie Viv nodded seriously. "Well, we may need it now."

Auntie Viv's flashing smile disappeared for a moment.

"'Ee, by 'eck, this sounds right serious. More dreams, Mattie. Or 'ave you seen Ben again?"

"Both!" answered Matthew.

"Right then. Sup up!" she ordered, handing them their mugs of tea. Then, "Let's 'ave it right from the beginning."

So, Matthew told her everything that had happened since they'd seen her last. The continuing dreams, becoming more and more vivid, the meeting with Ben, the two men. Then, finally, the very real delirious dream he'd had the day before.

"I don't like the sound of these two blokes," she said. "You're sure you don't know who they are?"

"I can never see their faces in my dream. That day in the wood their faces were covered too, weren't they?" Matthew looked at the other two for support and they nodded vigorously.

"And you're sure you know where Ben is?" Auntie Viv asked again.

"Yes, I'm positive," stated Matthew.

"Well, come on, then, there's nothing else for it."

88

"Where are we going?" asked Sophie.

"T'police station, down t'road. Bill Briggs is the sergeant down there now. 'E owes me a few favours, I've 'elped 'im out a few times wi' bits and bobs. 'E'll listen," Auntie Viv said, pulling on a long cardigan.

"They'll think we're mad!" said Russell. "Not even Mum and Dad would believe it. What hope will we have in convincing strangers?"

"If they think we're mad, they'll not be far wrong, will they me ol' flower?" laughed Auntie Viv, ushering them all out of her house. "Come on, we're off to find Ben!"

Matthew realised that they wouldn't have got very far without Auntie Viv, probably no further than the front desk of the police station in fact. She got them in to see Sergeant Briggs and they spoke to him in one of the interview rooms. He made it perfectly clear that he thought they were wasting his time.

"But, Viv! These are kids! They're probably making it up. I can't send men off to investigate this on a whim! Just because you say this lad dreamed about where Ben Walker is, doesn't mean I have to do something about it. I ask you, be serious."

"Fine!" said Auntie Viv who had listened to all this patiently, without butting in, even though she had wanted to. She picked up her bag as if to leave. "But, I'll tell you this, we're going to look anyway. What if we find him,

Bill? How will it look then? A bunch of kids uncovering a body the police searched about for weeks for and couldn't find? Tell me, what 'ave you got to lose? Come on, you owe me this, at least." She said all this looking straight at him.

"Oh, bloomin' 'eck. All right. Just let me get the details down of those two blokes you told me about, threatening the kids. Then I'll send a couple of police constables to go with you, this afternoon. But if this is a wild goose chase, I'll not be too pleased," he warned. Auntie Viv smiled, her famous flashing smile.

"Thanks, Bill," she said.

It was almost two o'clock when the party entered Wendles Wood. The PCs were very sour faced and disgruntled – they too felt this was a complete waste of time.

They each carried a shovel and walked behind Auntie Viv and the children. Layers of dead dried leaves crunched under their feet, even though there were still a lot of green leaves left on the trees.

They walked along and no one said a word. There was no sound other than the eerie silence and quietness of Ben's wood. As they all stepped into Oak Tree Clearing the heaviness of the wood seemed to lift from them a little.

"Which way, Mattie?" asked Auntie Viv. Matthew and Sophie both pointed down a path. The party set off once more along it.

"At the fork in the path, go left. There's a dip

just by the side of the pathway. Jump down and it's there," instructed Matthew.

As directed, they all went left at the fork. Matthew sniffed. The strong, earthy, peaty smell reached his nostrils. He looked around.

"Here!" he said, jumping from the path into a dip that ran alongside. "It's here!"

"Now, Mattie, are you sure?" nodded Auntie Viv.

"Yes," he answered confidently.

"Right, me ol' flowers," she turned to the constables, "roll up thy sleeves and start diggin'."

The policemen looked at each other, took off their coats and began to dig where Matthew had indicated. Matthew shivered. This place was just as he remembered it in his dream.

The policemen dug for a long time, the hole becoming deeper and deeper. At about five o'clock it was becoming almost impossible to see inside the wood. The policemen leaned on their shovels, wiped the sweat from their foreheads and shook their heads.

"There's nothing here, I'm afraid," one of them said.

"Can we try again, tomorrow?" asked Matthew, beginning to feel worried. He knew they were close, now. He could feel it in his bones.

"I don't think we'll be coming back here," the other policeman remarked, switching on his torch.

"Just another five mins, eh chaps?" cajoled Auntie Viv.

The policemen shook their heads again, but started digging anyway.

"Five minutes it is, missus!" mumbled one of them.

"You'd all best be off 'ome, me little flowers. There's nowt you can do 'ere. I'll wait with these young blokes. Go on, now. See you later," she called sadly.

Matthew, Russell and Sophie didn't want to go.

"Come on, Matt. Mum and Dad will be worried." Russell pulled Matthew away and clambered out of the ditch. The three of them began to walk back towards Oak Tree Clearing. Their heads hung low, especially Matthew's. He'd been so sure, so certain.

They stepped into the clearing. Ben was sitting on a tree stump with his head in his hands, waiting.

"Ben!" shouted Matthew, running over to him. "I nearly didn't see you in our torchlight."

Russell and Sophie both jumped.

"Ben, we couldn't find you!" Matthew practically sobbed with disappointment.

"You're close," said Ben weakly. "I feel really weird. You must be very close."

"Where is he, then?" asked Russell.

"He's here!" Matthew turned to answer his brother. He gestured at Ben, but when he had turned back, Ben had gone. "Well, he was here..."

There was a sudden shout from along the path where Auntie Viv and the policemen were.

"Soph, Mattie, Russ! Come back. We've got something, I think! Come back! Quickly!"

They dashed back along the path, stumbling over their feet and practically falling over one another. When they reached the dip by the side of the path, the policemen were shining their torches at the side of the deep hole it had taken them all afternoon to dig.

"Some earth fell in from t'side. Just 'ere, look!" pointed Auntie Viv. "Just loose earth, but just look what it's uncovered. I 'ope you've got strong stomachs."

The policemen shone both of their torches onto the area that Auntie Viv was indicating. They all made out, quite clearly, two fingers of a skeletal hand.

"Yes!" whispered Matthew. Russell and Sophie looked at it in disbelief.

"Yuk!" said Russell, turning away as nausea overcame him.

"Well, I'll be...!" the policemen were still shaking their heads in disbelief. Auntie Viv took charge.

"Now, let's leave these officers to do their jobs, shall we?"

Matthew opened his mouth to protest, he desperately wanted to stay.

"No, Mattie, no arguin'. There's nowt else we can do 'ere. We found 'im and that's what we were 'ere for. Come on, your mum and dad will be tearin' out their 'air wi' worry."

She ushered the three of them away. As they

walked down the path they all heard the policemen on their radios asking for back up assistance and explaining just exactly what they believed they'd uncovered.

When they got back to the campsite, it was completely dark. Matthew and Russell ran over to their caravan to find no one there. They started to panic.

"Mum and dad must be out looking for us!" Russell said.

"Wait 'til they find out what we've done!"

"Come up t'farmhouse, lads," Auntie Viv said. "We'll leave a note on t'door for your mum and dad to say where you are."

They walked over the campsite to Sophie's farmhouse, only to meet the boys' mum and dad coming the other way. They were huddled together looking frightened. As soon as they saw their sons, looks of relief softened their faces and they ran over to hug them both. Then their mum clipped them both lightly round the ear.

"Where have you been? We've been worried sick. We just went to see if you were at Sophie's. Sophie's mum's just ringing her aunt."

"Er, that'll be me," said Auntie Viv. "Your boys were fine. They were with me, but I know it's late. There's a good reason, though. I think you'd better come on up t'house. There's quite a lot of explaining to do."

"Mum, you'll never guess..." began Russell, bursting to tell his parents about what had happened. He'd been jigging about all the time

94

the adults were talking.

"Russ, wait, me flower. You'll only confuse your mum and dad. Let them 'ear the whole lot!"

The party followed Auntie Viv into the brightly lit farmhouse. Sophie shut the door.

Chapter 15

Two hours later everyone came out of the house. They were all wrapped up and carrying torches. Matthew's dad had his arm around his mum and they walked along together, shaking their heads occasionally. Sophie's parents were with them too. All of them set off towards the wood, torches flashing this way and that like a laser show.

Matthew walked along in the middle of the group with Russell and Sophie at his side. They entered the wood. With so many of them trampling along, the wood suddenly felt less eerie. They all felt safe in each other's company. Matthew knew it would have been a different story, if each of them had been alone. When they reached Oak Tree Clearing, all of them could hear a commotion to their left.

"Aye, down this way," pointed Auntie Viv and they all followed.

Even before they got to the fork in the path, they were able to switch off their torches. The whole area was lit up like a Christmas tree. It had been floodlit and it was as bright as day — well, brighter than day in that part of the wood, which was always so grey and dismal. White tape with 'POLICE CORDON' written on it was wrapped around the trees and it totally surrounded the dip at the side of the path. Policemen stood around the cordon, almost on guard. There was a tent over the place where Ben's body had been found. It was impossible to see anything.

"We can't get through. It's hopeless," said Matthew.

"You're right!" Russell added. "Hang on, isn't that the Sergeant we spoke to today? Sergeant Briggs?" He pointed to a group of policemen hovering about by the dip.

"Aye, well done, Russ," Auntie Viv slapped Russell heartily on the back, then called, "Bill? Bill? Over 'ere, Sergeant Briggs."

Sergeant Briggs shielded his eyes against the brightness of the lights and peered through the trees to see who was calling him. He recognised them, waved, then started across to them.

"What's happening, Sergeant?" Sophie's dad asked. "We've just heard a very bizarre story from my sister-in-law, here. Is it true?"

Sergeant Briggs looked around at them all.

"We can't say yet sir," he said cagily, looking over his shoulder. "It's been taken out of our hands, now. The CID have been brought in. No doubt you'll be able to read the full story in the newspaper. Obviously we'll need to interview the children, but I've asked them to leave that until the morning."

"Now, you wait one minute, Billy Briggs!" Auntie Viv barged through angrily. "If it 'adn't been for Mattie 'ere, you'd have found nothing! Now, you tell us what's goin' on."

Sergeant Briggs took off his hat and ran his

fingers through his hair. His voice dropped almost to a whisper. "We've found the remains of a body," he said solemnly. "The pathologist has just finished a preliminary examination."

"And?" asked Auntie Viv.

"Well, we won't know whether it's Ben Walker or not until tomorrow. We have to check dental records, but…"

"But what?" they all leaned forward to hear what he was saying.

"But the pathologist has said that from the looks of the skeleton, it's a male, approximate age fifteen. There were also a few scraps of material found under the body. Bits of blue denim and black cotton. We were lucky to find those, the soil can't be too acidic here."

"It's him," whispered Matthew. "It's Ben. Where is he?" Matthew said loudly. "Has he gone? Have you taken him away?"

The Sergeant frowned at Matthew's tendency to talk of Ben as if he was very much alive.

"We have the remains on a stretcher, near to the police van. Just over there," indicated the Sergeant.

The whole group peered through the trees. Something that looked like a black plastic sleeping bag was lying on a stretcher, ready to be loaded into the police van and taken away.

"I never said goodbye," said Matthew. Auntie Viv pulled him over to her side.

"Let him through, Bill," she ordered.

"I can't," he hissed, "I told you, it's out of our

98

hands now."

At that moment flashlights seemed to go off all over the wood. Sergeant Briggs groaned.

"Sorry, Viv. The press have got hold of it. Didn't take them long! I'll have to go and sort it out. Go home, now, all of you. We'll be in touch in the morning. We'll need the children to give statements."

He waved them away and they all went reluctantly. Except for Matthew. He stood at the cordon gripping the tape tightly and staring at the stretcher. The stretcher with Ben on it.

"Matthew, come on!" called his mum. He turned to follow them, but something to the right of him caught his eye. He walked a little way out of the light and stopped. There, standing behind a tree, was Ben.

Auntie Viv turned to see where Matthew was, then ushered the others on.

"He's coming now," she called, "you go on. I'll wait for 'im." She waved at Matthew.

Ben smiled and put out his hand. Matthew did the same. They stood for a moment smiling and shaking hands silently. There was something different about Ben, but Matthew couldn't make out what.

"I don't know what to say Matt," Ben said.

"It's all right. I'm just glad we found you," Matthew replied.

"I would never have been found, if not for you," Ben said.

"Well, you told me where to look."

"No, I don't think I did," frowned Ben.

"Who did then?" asked Matthew.

"Who knows?" smiled Ben. "You're pretty in tune with what's going on this side, you know."

"Yes," laughed Matthew, not really sure what Ben meant.

"Anyway, I can go now. I'm not stuck here any more. I can say a proper goodbye. Thanks."

"I'm glad I had the chance to see you before you went," said Matthew, smiling.

"Me too," said Ben. "I must go now, Matt. Thanks for everything. Make sure you get justice for me, eh?"

Matthew nodded, knowing that Ben was talking about the two men. They had left him there, in the wood, for three years. Then, he suddenly realised what was different.

"Where's your scar? Above your eye?" he asked Ben.

Ben felt above his eye and across to his temple. He smiled again.

"It's healed. At last."

There was a clattering and clanging as the policemen loaded the stretcher into the police van. Matthew watched it go in. As he turned back Ben seemed to be fading before his eyes. He waved and mouthed 'Bye' and Matthew did the same. Then he was gone.

Auntie Viv was waiting on the path for him.

"I'm glad you got the chance to see 'im before 'e went," she said.

"Me, too," Matthew replied.

"'E was a good lookin' lad, nice bit of beef, like thee!" she remarked, digging him in the ribs.

"You saw him?" he asked.

"Aye, lad, I did," she answered as they walked through Oak Tree Clearing to join the others.

Chapter 16

The families spent almost the whole of the next day at the village police station. Sergeant Briggs had telephoned Auntie Viv and Sophie's parents and had asked the Jardines to be at the police station for ten o'clock that morning.

Bill Briggs interviewed the children with Auntie Viv present. Even though she was their adult chaperone, and had to be there while the police talked to the children, everyone knew that there would have been no keeping her out.

Once in the interview room the tape was switched on to record whatever was said. Matthew, Russell and Sophie began to tell their story.

It was Matthew who did most of the talking, backed up occasionally by Russell, Sophie or Auntie Viv. Auntie Viv tended to butt in, particularly when Matthew mentioned his dreams or his sightings of Ben. The police were obviously very sceptical, but said nothing. Their sideways glances at each other were proof enough. Auntie Viv wanted Matthew to know he had her support.

"The last thing Ben said to me was that he wanted justice done," Matthew said, and Auntie Viv nodded in agreement. "I think," went on Matthew, "that he meant he wanted you to catch the two youths in the wood. I know that they didn't actually kill Ben, but one

102

of them shot him. They buried his body, too."

"Yes," said Sergeant Briggs. "They must have been scared. Thought they'd be in the clear if no one could find the body. They were, too, for three years!"

The door opened and another policeman walked into the room.

"Can I have a word, Sarge?" he said. The Sergeant left the room with him. After about ten minutes he came back.

"We've identified the body," he said. Everyone looked at him. Matthew held his breath. At last, confirmation that he wasn't mad! "It was Ben Walker."

The children and Auntie Viv closed their eyes. Matthew was right.

"We've contacted Ben's family to inform them that we have found their son. They needed to know before the story hits the papers. It'll probably make the Nationals."

"What did Ben's family say?" asked Sophie.

"I'm not sure. I should think it came as a bit of a shock, though, after all these years. They did say that they would come up. They want to see where Ben was found."

"Well, that's only natural," said Auntie Viv. "'E was there a right long time."

"The newspapers will want to talk to you three, I should imagine," the Sergeant said to them. They nodded. "I think it would be better to conduct that as a small press conference. We'll read out a statement and then answer questions as best we can."

"Why do you want to do it like that?" asked Auntie Viv.

"I think it's best to play down Matthew's dreams and sightings of Ben. After all, the press would have a field day with that. You'd get a lot of unwelcome attention, Matthew. It's too contentious. Plus a lot of it was coincidence, you must admit."

Auntie Viv tutted loudly.

"I've been up against this before, Mattie. People are scared of things they don't understand. Don't worry, me ol' flower," she soothed.

Matthew looked around at the others.

"I know what you mean. Not even my own parents believed me. They wanted to, I think, but they were frightened. It took Russ a while too, didn't it?"

Russell nodded his agreement and Sergeant Briggs turned off the tape.

"That's it, then. We have descriptions of these two men. We'll be keeping a close eye out for them. They're bound to surface when all this hits the papers."

They all had lunch at the police station canteen. Both sets of parents were brought up to date with everything that had gone on that morning. Mr and Mrs Jardine kept looking over at their eldest son thoughtfully. They saw him in a totally new light.

Matthew, Russell and Sophie chatted normally, taking every new experience in their stride, as usual.

Sergeant Briggs arranged the press conference for after lunch. Only a select handful of journalists had been invited and they were all herded into an interview room beforehand.

Sergeant Briggs sat with the children and their families in another room and read out the statement he was about to give. It was short and to the point.

"'At 5.15pm yesterday, the body of Ben Walker, who has been listed as a missing person for three years, was recovered from Wendles Wood. The police would like to extend their thanks to Matthew Jardine for information leading to the recovery. It has been confirmed that Ben, aged fourteen, died from a fall causing a serious skull fracture. His next of kin have been notified.' That's it." Sergeant Briggs said, looking around at them all.

"Well, they won't be satisfied with that. Not one bit, Bill," said Auntie Viv, folding her arms across her chest.

As it turned out, she was right.

They all sat at the back of one of the larger rooms in the police station to watch what happened at the press conference. As soon as the statement had been read, every journalist there shouted out a question.

"How did Matthew help? What's his involvement?" shouted one.

"Where exactly was Ben found?" called another.

"Wendles Wood!" someone called out the answer.

"Are there any suspicious circumstances?"

"What did this Matthew do?"

"What made you reopen the investigation?"

Sergeant Briggs banged the table.

"Ben Walker's body was found inside Wendles Wood. We would like to question two men about his disappearance."

"But how is Matthew involved?" shouted a lone female voice.

"Matthew found evidence that led us to reopen the investigation," Sergeant Briggs answered.

"What evidence?" called the same voice.

"He found Ben's handkerchief."

There were gasps of disbelief and murmurs of, "After three years!" and "Impossible!" rang around the room.

"Why didn't the police find it three years ago, when the police combed those woods looking for Ben?" she said.

"The handkerchief was found by pure accident. We were very lucky it was so well preserved. Now, thank you ladies and gentlemen, that's all."

Sergeant Briggs pushed back his chair and slowly got to his feet.

"We need more photographs, is that possible?" shouted someone from the back.

"Yes, of course. I'll make the arrangements," Sergeant Briggs nodded.

"Could we do it now? At Wendles Wood, at

the place where Ben was found?" the female voice called out.

"Could we take Matthew and his friends with us?" someone else called. The Sergeant looked over to Matthew, Russell and Sophie questioningly. Matthew nodded that he wouldn't mind.

"That would be acceptable," the Sergeant agreed, "I'll see what I can do."

A little while later, a convoy of cars passed through the village and swept up to Wendles Wood. Once at the edge of Stile Copse, everyone got out and trekked the half an hour walk to where Ben's body had been found.

The police cordon had been taken down. The group stood around staring at the rectangle of freshly dug earth. It looked like a grave now. Someone had put flowers on it. A big bunch. The photographers took lots of photographs of them. Flashlights stung everyone's eyes.

"Can we have one of the kids? Matthew and his friends in front of the grave?" shouted someone. Matthew squirmed. They were so detached, they couldn't have cared less about Ben. All they were after was a good story, the bloodier and more gruesome the better. They made him angry.

Matthew, Russell and Sophie were bundled forward. Matthew was frowning.

"I'm not his friend, I'm his brother!" Russell hissed angrily. He didn't like their attitude either.

Sophie stood beside them, looking very solemn.

"This is worse than one of my nightmares!" Matthew whispered to them.

"Enough, now," shouted Sergeant Briggs. "That's your lot, I'm afraid, ladies and gentlemen."

"Rev up and bog off!" called Auntie Viv.

The families started to laugh, as the press left in dribs and drabs. They were all after just one more photograph. But at last they were gone.

"Do you all want a lift back?" Sergeant Briggs asked the group. Auntie Viv nodded.

"It's quicker for us to walk. Thanks anyway," said Matthew's dad.

"Thanks, we'll do the same," added Sophie's mum.

"Well, thank you all for your help. We'll be in touch."

The group split. Matthew lagged behind for one last look at Ben's grave. He knew he would never come back here again. It was over.

A twig snapped behind the dip, but in front of where he was standing. He peered through the trees, but could see nothing. He had an uncomfortable feeling though. Someone was watching him. He was sure of it.

He followed the noise a little way.

"Come on, Matt!" Russell called.

Matthew turned back to follow the noise. He just caught a glimpse of a figure slipping away. It was a boy, around about the same size as he

108

was. He was wearing jeans and a black T-shirt and he had shaggy blonde hair.

Matthew stopped dead in his tracks. If he didn't know better, he would have sworn that he'd just seen Ben...

Chapter 17

The next morning the local *Guardian* had the recovery of Ben's body splashed all over the front page. Matthew's dad had been out early to buy a copy. Matthew and Russell dashed to the paper and unfolded it. There was a picture of them, together with Sophie looking very sombre.

"Ha, ha! Look at your face!" laughed Russell, pointing at Matthew's photograph with glee.

"I'd take a look at yours before you poke fun!" answered his brother.

"Ooo, errr. Yes, you're right!" Russell giggled.

"We all look absolutely awful. Listen to what it says..."

Russell read out the article. As well as describing when, where and how Ben was found, there was also a scathing attack on the local police force.

"They want to know how a fourteen year old and two twelve year olds can do in one week, what the police couldn't do in three years."

"That's not really fair," said Matthew.

"There's not a lot that is fair in this life, Matt," said his dad.

"I wonder if Sophie's seen this awful picture? It looks as if she's about to burst into tears," giggled Russell.

Matthew looked over Russell's shoulder.

"She looks like a startled rabbit," he said. "Come on, we'll go and show it to her. Is that okay, Mum?"

His mum nodded.

"No going into that wood, though, do you hear?" she mumbled through a piece of toast.

The two brothers pulled on their jackets and trainers and headed off towards the farmhouse, armed with the local *Guardian*.

"Do you mind not getting any of the credit, Matt?" Russell asked as they walked.

"What do you mean?" Matthew said.

"Well, finding Ben was all down to you. It had nothing to do with us or the police. Yet you're getting nothing out of it at all."

"Yes, I am," replied Matthew. "We found Ben and that's all I set out to do. We couldn't have told everyone the whole truth, they'd have thought we were daft! Mum and Dad made me realise that when we tried to tell them what was happening. There's not much chance of anyone else believing you, when your parents don't, is there?"

"I see what you mean," nodded Russell. "Still, it doesn't seem fair."

"It doesn't matter, Ben's been found. End of story," Matthew said.

"But what about finding the men?" asked Russell. "It's not the end until they've been caught." He shuddered and looked around quickly, remembering how scared he'd been last time they had shown up. "They'll read this in the papers. It says the police want to interview two men seen in the vicinity around the time of Ben's disappearance. It says a new witness has come forward with startling new evidence. I hope they don't come after us."

"Shut up, Russ," said Matthew, knocking on Sophie's door. Russell nudged his brother in the ribs with his elbow. Matthew jostled him back. Then the door opened.

The two brothers looked at each other, standing open mouthed at the person who stood before them.

"Yes?" he said. Matthew was too flabbergasted to speak. The boy before him was about his age and size. He had shaggy blonde hair, deep blue eyes and he was wearing a black T-shirt and blue jeans.

"You look just like the photo I saw of Ben Walker," Russell piped up. The boy smiled.

Matthew was still staring at the boy, waiting for a flicker of recognition to pass over the boy's face when he looked at him. But none did. The boy still didn't speak.

"We've come for Sophie," said Russell, "Is she in?"

"You're her friends," the boy said at last. "The ones in this morning's newspaper. Matt and Russ?"

"Yes," said Russell.

"Come in, I'll get her," he motioned for them to come inside. "By the way, I'm John Walker, Ben's brother."

Matthew watched his face as they went in. There was something different about this lad, but they were also uncannily similar.

"Were you in the wood, yesterday?" Matthew asked. John frowned for a fleeting second. "When the press were there. At the place where Ben was found?"

"Yes, I was. I thought you'd spotted me. We had, well, that is me and my mum and dad, we'd been to see the place where Ben was found. Mum wanted to leave some flowers. Then you lot turned up. We couldn't face it, questions and photographs. It's been quite a shock, you know. It's dredged up all those horrible feelings I felt three years ago."

"Yes, I can imagine," Matthew said sympathetically.

"Can you?" snapped John.

"Sorry," said Matthew quietly.

They walked into the lounge. It was bright, with large windows that let in a lot of light. Sophie was sitting on the sofa with her parents. A man and woman sat opposite them.

"Matt! Russ!" Sophie jumped up, pleased to see them. "I was just coming across to call for you. I wanted you to meet Mr and Mrs Walker, Ben's mum and dad," she added quietly.

"Hello." Matthew and Russell smiled politely. Mrs Walker put out her hand and they went over to shake it.

"You must be Matthew," she said to him. "You're the one who found Ben's handkerchief, the one I sent Ben's photograph to."

"Yes," Matthew replied.

"Thank you so much." Mr Walker stood up.

"The police would never have reopened the case without your evidence. We're very grateful."

Matthew nodded, slightly embarrassed. Ben's brother was watching him carefully. There was an awkward silence.

"Have you seen the paper?" asked Russell. Matthew glared at him.

"John has, but we couldn't bear to look," said Mrs Walker. "We just want an end to it now. We want Ben to be able to rest in peace."

"The police think two men may be responsible for Ben's death. I'd like to see them caught and brought to justice," said John angrily. "Then that'll be an end to it."

"Ben felt the same," Matthew nodded. Everyone turned to look at him and Matthew realised what he'd said, but too late. He added, "I should imagine," to cover his mistake.

"We're taking Ben home, the day after tomorrow. Give him a proper funeral. Say goodbye properly." Mrs Walker's voice cracked and her husband put his arm around her.

"We'd be glad if you could come," she added tearfully.

Russell looked horrified. They'd never been to a funeral before. Matthew, though, stayed very calm.

"We'd need to ask my parents," he said. Mr and Mrs Walker nodded and smiled.

"Can I go out for a while?" asked Sophie.

"For ten minutes," her mum said.

"Coming, John?" she asked breezily.

"No thanks," he replied, still watching Matthew.

Matthew was finding it very difficult to avoid looking at John. He was so much like Ben.

The three of them went outside into Sophie's yard. Matthew was very quiet.

"He's the dead spit of Ben, isn't he Matt?" said Sophie. Matthew nodded.

"It was a bit of a shock seeing him at your front door," Matthew remarked.

"He's okay though," Sophie went on. "The whole family are naturally a bit shaken up by this. They're staying with us. Mum said it was the least we could do."

"We came to show you this awful picture of us all," Russell said, grabbing the paper from under Matthew's arm and unfolding it.

"Oh, yuk!" Sophie pulled a face. "We look like the three wise monkeys!"

"What?" asked Russell.

"Nothing, just something Auntie Viv would say. I'm not sure what it means! I'd best go back in. Mum doesn't like me to be out when we've got people visiting," she shrugged her shoulders apologetically. "See you after lunch, then. I'll try to get John to come, as well."

"Yes, see you," called Matthew and Russell, by now halfway down the path.

Chapter 18

Sophie didn't call for them that afternoon. Matthew and Russell hadn't really expected her to. The brothers spent the rest of the day playing cards and watching TV. Russell asked Matthew to go out countless times, but Matthew shook his head.

"I want to stay in," he kept saying, "I'm tired."

Russell waited patiently and hoped that Sophie would come over after all. Perhaps she would be able to get Matthew to change his mind. But she never came.

Russell knew that Matthew was acting strangely. It wasn't like him to stay in, he was usually the one wanting to get out.

It was dark by half past five and Russell was totally fed up.

"Well, that was a real waste of a day's holiday," he mumbled crossly, unable to keep quiet any longer.

"What?" Matthew asked, not looking at him and only half listening to him. "What did you say?"

"Why didn't you want to go out today? We could have gone into the village. Or we could have gone swimming. Or just a walk!" Russell moaned.

Matthew shifted about on his seat.

"Shut up!" he said. He knew Russell was right. He had wanted to go out too, but he had a lot of things on his mind. Mainly the two men in Wendles Wood.

"Why wouldn't you come out? Were you waiting for Sophie? Can't we do anything without her, anymore?" Russell went on. He knew full well that talking to Matthew like this would lead to a row. He also felt guilty because he knew this wasn't really Sophie's fault. It was Matthew he was mad at! After everything that had happened in the last few days – all the excitement, today had fallen totally flat.

"Don't be stupid!" said Matthew, trying to keep calm.

"It's got nothing to do with Sophie."

"Why, then? Why have we been stuck in here all day?" Russell asked.

Matthew gave him a filthy look and continued to sit in a brooding silence. He didn't know how to explain to Russell how he was feeling. He felt as though there was a brick at the pit of his stomach. He knew that something was going to happen. He also knew that it wasn't going to be anything good. At last Matthew mumbled, "If you must know it's because of those two men."

Russell turned to look at his brother.

"What?"

"Those two men. I'm worried about what they'll do. They know who we are, Russ. Ben's recovery was splashed all over the paper this morning," Matthew went on. "The two men were mentioned in the story."

"So?" said Russell.

"So, they threatened to come after us. If they're going to, now's the time they'll do it. We know too much. We saw them in the wood and the police are looking for two men who fit their description. They know we're bound to go to the police and say that we saw them a few days ago. I've been thinking about it all day. The more I've thought, the more I know it makes sense to keep our heads down. We've got to keep out of their way. Stay out of sight. Otherwise, I've got this feeling that something terrible is going to happen. We need to lie low until we get home."

Russell listened carefully to all Matthew had to say.

"But what about Sophie? The men know she was with us. What happens when we go off home? They might go after her," he said.

"Perhaps, but we can't do anything about that. I don't see that we have any other option," Matthew mumbled.

Russell stood up angrily. "I can't believe you've just said that. Sophie's our friend. Well, I'll tell you something, shall I? I'm not staying cooped up in this caravan for the rest of the holiday looking at you sulking. You can stay here if you like, but I'd rather be out there, trying to see if I can find out who these men are. Doing what Ben asked you to do, trying to bring them to justice." Russell glared at his brother, feeling let down and disappointed in him. His brother had never backed away from anything in his life before. It was so unlike him.

"Shut up, you're giving me a headache," Matthew said flatly. Russell marched out of the lounge and into the bedroom. Matthew shifted around in his seat again. He was confused and tired. What should they do? Lie low and keep safe, or was Russell right? Should they try to find out who the two men were?

His mum and dad were surprised when both of their sons were in bed by eight o'clock.

"Where are you going?" his dad asked when Matthew went to get washed and ready for bed.

"Bed," he said flatly. His mum and dad looked at each other in disbelief, eyebrows raised questioningly.

"Are you okay Matt?" his mum asked.

"Fine," he answered. "Just a bit tired, that's all."

"Russ must be tired too. He nipped in to say goodnight while you were in the loo a while ago."

Russell had gone to bed first and when Matthew came into the bedroom, he pretended to be fast asleep.

Sophie came to call for them the next morning. Matthew and Russell still weren't speaking to each other and there was a frosty chill between them as Sophie walked into the lounge.

"Hello!" she smiled at them, in her bright and breezy way. She was hardly acknowledged by the boys, who barely managed to grunt hello between them. "Are you coming out? John's not all that keen," she added.

"He's not the only one," Russell said, glaring at his brother.

"What's up?" she asked.

"It's Matthew. He's scared of the men. Thinks we should lie low and hide from them. We've got to stay locked up in this caravan forever!" Russell replied dramatically. Matthew ignored him. Sophie started to giggle, then stopped suddenly as she remembered something.

"Oh, by the way, there was a terrible business in the village yesterday." Both brothers looked at her. "Do you remember Mrs Cowling who we went to see with the baby?" They nodded. "Well, somebody smashed all of her windows, then posted a lighted rag soaked with petrol through the letterbox!"

"Was anyone hurt?" asked Russell.

"I don't think so. They put the fire out quickly, but it caused a lot of damage to the house, especially downstairs," she said.

"Was the baby all right? Did they manage to get out without anyone getting hurt?" Russell asked again.

"Well, the baby was asleep in the bedroom when the windows smashed. Some splinters of glass caught him on the forehead. I don't think it was anything serious though," Sophie replied.

"How awful!" said Matthew. "Was everyone else okay?"

"Yes. The police went round though. They were there ages according to Auntie Viv. No

120

one saw anything of course. They haven't got a clue who did it."

The three of them sat staring into the pattern in the carpet for a while and said nothing.

"Are you coming out then?" Sophie asked at last. Matthew shook his head and shifted about uneasily in his seat. He still didn't know what to do.

"I really don't think we ought to," he said seriously.

"Well, nuts to you! I'm coming, Soph." Russell jumped up and pulled down his jacket from the peg in the tiny hallway. "Come on, let's leave old mardy misery guts here!"

Matthew pulled a face at him. Sophie and Russell walked to the front door.

"What's this?" asked Sophie, bending over and picking up a white envelope which was lying on the mat. "Someone's left you a love letter!" she teased. Matthew got up and came over to take a look. Russell took the letter from her.

"No name on it, so I'll open it. Might be too dangerous for you to open, Matt! Might be a letter bomb! Or the two men from the wood might be inside waiting to jump out at you! Whooo!"

"Shut up, pea brain! You're not funny."

Russell tore at the envelope, then opened the piece of folded paper inside and read,

"Will meet you in Oak Tree Clearing, about 10.30am. John."

"It's only from John," Sophie sounded a little disappointed. "He must have changed his mind." She looked at her watch. "Come on, we'll just make it. Are you sure you won't come, Matt?" she pleaded.

"I don't think you ought to go into the wood, especially not Oak Tree Clearing," warned Matthew. "I've got a funny feeling."

"Oh, take a tablet then. Perhaps your funny feeling will go away. Let's leave him."

Russell pulled her out of the door impatiently. "Bye, then!" he shouted to his mum and dad who were in the kitchen. He heard a muffled reply from them. Matthew watched them go with a growing sense of unease. He had that sinking feeling back in the pit of his stomach and it was getting much worse. He walked back slowly into the lounge, holding the note from John. Suddenly he felt a blinding flash of light shoot across the top of his forehead. He closed his eyes to shut out the pain and had to steady himself by leaning against the television. He thought he was going to pass out. An image burst into his mind. It was fuzzy at first, but slowly it came into focus. Then Matthew could see the picture as clear as day. It was the two men. They were standing in the wood in Oak Tree Clearing. Another blinding flash shot through his head. Matthew steadied himself and the picture was gone.

He sat down, a little shaken. He held his head in his hands. Then it suddenly hit him.

How did John know about the locals' name for the clearing? Why hadn't he just knocked on the caravan door to tell them that he had changed his mind about coming out? Why had that picture of the two men just flashed into his head, as clear as a bell? Something was wrong. Very wrong.

Without thinking he pulled on his jacket and shouted, "I'm off out a minute!" to his parents. He ran across to the farmhouse, looking towards the wood to see if he could still see Russell or Sophie, but they'd gone. He shouted their names loudly hoping they would hear him. Then they might stop and come back. But they were nowhere to be seen. A feeling of panic crept up from his toes. He started to run towards the wood, thinking that he might catch them up before they got too far. Then he realised that they would have run most of the way themselves. The note had said that John would meet them at 10.30am. He looked at his watch. It was 10.32am. He stopped and spun round, running back the way he had come. He wanted desperately to be wrong about this. He hoped it would be all right. The blood pumped in his head. He looked around frantically. There was something wrong, he knew it!

He had an awful feeling that John hadn't sent the note after all, and he wanted to check. He ran up the path and banged hard on the brass knocker. The door opened. Matthew's suspicions were confirmed. John stood there, looking at him with a puzzled expression. As soon as he saw Matthew's face, he knew something was the matter.

"What's up?" he asked at once.

Chapter 19

Russell and Sophie had made good time tramping through the wood. They'd been playing tag most of the time and they were out of breath when, giggling, they practically fell into the clearing.

They looked around. Sophie glanced down at her watch, "It's only 10.35," she said.

"We're not that late."

"He's not here," Russell said.

"Perhaps he's a little way off, down one of the paths?" Sophie suggested. "John?" she called. "Yoooo hoooo! John?"

Russell began to giggle. They looked in every direction.

"Oh well, never mind. We'll go back, shall we? How do you fancy going swimming this afternoon?" he asked.

Sophie nodded and then shouted, "John?" once more.

"He must have changed his mind, again," said Russell.

"Come on, I'll race you! Swimming pool here we come."

The two of them began to run out of the clearing, down the path home. A sharp crack above them splintered the heavy quietness of the wood and stopped them in their tracks. They turned around quickly to see where the sound had come from.

"What was that?" said Sophie, startled.

Two men were standing in the clearing, with guns raised to their shoulders. The guns were pointing straight at them. It had been a gun shot that they had heard.

One of the men fired at them again. Russell and Sophie ducked down and stayed down, too frightened to move...

"That was over your heads, the next ones are aimed right at you!" one of the men shouted.

"Get back here!" the other man ordered.

Russell and Sophie slowly got up from their crouched position and walked back to the clearing. They knew it would be pointless calling for help, no one would hear them. Russell began to wish that he'd listened to his brother.

Sophie was shaking.

"Russ, I'm scared," she whispered.

"Matt was right!" Russell whispered back. "Don't worry, though. It'll be all right," he said softly. He was frightened, too, but he wasn't going to let on.

As the children approached the men, they realised they were the same men who had chased them through the wood a few days ago. They wore hoods still, so that Sophie and Russell couldn't see their faces properly. They were wearing large overcoats and black wellingtons.

"Now, what have we here?" one of them said menacingly.

"Where's the other one?"

Russell and Sophie exchanged glances.

"I said, where's the other one?" the man leaned forward and shouted at their faces. They both drew back as he raised his gun. They thought he was going to hit Russell over the head with the butt end of it.

Sophie shouted, "He decided not to come. He stayed at home."

The men backed off a little, huddled together and whispered to each other.

"Well, we've got a little message for all three of you," one said.

"We've been watching you, see. We know where you live and we know Ben Walker's family are staying with you."

Sophie had one of the guns poked in her stomach.

"That's how we got you here, just by watching. Patiently watching," the other one carried on, almost snarling at them.

"You keep quiet about us. If the police ask you if you've seen us, you keep your traps shut! Do you hear me?" They leaned over the two of them again, threateningly. Russell and Sophie nodded their heads quickly.

"If you go to the police, we might have to smash all your windows, or warm your house up a bit. Understand?"

Sophie glanced across quickly to Russell. She did understand, now. She understood only too well.

"We want to leave you with a little warning. A memento of what's to come if you don't do as you're told. If either you, or the other one blabs, you get this!" They waved the barrels of the guns in the children's faces.

They backed away a good few metres, pulled up the guns to their shoulders and took aim. Russell and Sophie could see full well that the guns were aimed at their legs. Russell closed his eyes, sure that they meant to shoot one of them. He waited for the 'crack' of the gun.

Sophie shouted, "No!" and covered her eyes with her hands.

But no gun was fired. There was a sound. A sound of grappling and of a fierce struggle, but there was no gun shot. Russell and Sophie opened their eyes in surprise. The noise and the thuds which were followed by loud groans, were the result of the two men being rugby tackled from behind. It was the last thing they were expecting and both of them went down like a ton of bricks. Their guns flew out of their hands and fell a few metres in front of them.

Both Matthew and John had gone in hard together with their right shoulders and hit the men just behind the knees, holding on to the men's legs tightly and for all they were worth...

Matthew had heard something 'pop' as he hit his man. He wasn't sure if it was his shoulder or the man's knee. Either way, he didn't care. They were about to shoot his brother. He had to do something. The men hit the ground almost face first, earth flying up into their eyes, a thud as they landed heavily on the earth and both guns

128

dropped in surprise.

After the initial shock, things happened quickly. Sophie and Russell dashed forward to grab the guns, Russell shouting, "Ah, ha!" at the men as he did so.

John and Matthew jumped up as the men realised what had happened and scrambled to their feet, still a little bewildered. One of them was hopping about, holding his knee.

"What the devil...?" one of them shouted, obviously in pain.

Sophie and Russell raised the guns. Russell said, "Have some of that, then! Oh, by the way, stick 'em up!" he smiled, mimicking his favourite TV superhero.

Matthew and John stood and faced the men squarely. They were both ready to fight if they had to. The men saw that.

They looked at the two boys in front of them, they looked behind at the guns pointed at them. Then they looked at each other.

"He's flamin' well knocked my knee out, Jack!" shouted the one that was still hopping about.

"You're all dead!" the other one snarled.

For one awful minute Matthew thought the man was about to lunge at them. It was obvious he was thinking about it. But just at that moment, like a cavalry charge, their fathers came crashing through the wood into the clearing. Sophie's dad had a gun and took charge immediately. It didn't take them long to weigh up the situation.

"So, these are the cowards that have been threatening my twelve year old daughter," he said angrily, striding towards them. John's dad restrained him. "Okay, it's okay. We've got them now," he soothed.

The men stood still and began to cower a little. Their hands were slightly raised in a position of surrender.

"These are the two men the police want to question. They were in the wood, the evening Ben disappeared, Dad," Sophie called.

Matthew nodded. He knew they were the men in his dreams but he couldn't tell them that. They'd have thought he was crazy.

Everyone looked at Sophie for an explanation.

"I'm certain these are the men and I think I can prove it too," she went on.

"I think it's a trip to the police station, gentlemen," said John's dad, marching towards them menacingly. Now Sophie's dad had to step in to stop tempers flaring any further. "It's okay. We've got them Bill," he said. John's dad nodded.

"But they were probably the last ones to see my son alive," he said quietly.

The fathers turned to the children. "Well handled all of you. Although I told you, Matthew, to wait for us."

"You too, John," Mr Walker said.

"Sorry, Dad," Matthew and John said together, knowing that they would have been too late if they had waited.

"You four go back and tell your mothers what's happened. We'll meet you at the police station as soon as you're able to get there, okay?" said Sophie's dad.

The fathers took the guns from Russell and Sophie, who gave them up reluctantly. Then the two villains were led roughly down the path. One of them was still hobbling quite badly and complaining all the way about his knee.

John, Matthew, Russell and Sophie walked behind. They were a little shaken by what had happened.

"How come you knew you had to follow us?" Russell began.

"I realised John didn't know the local name for Oak Tree Clearing. By the time I'd twigged, I tried to follow you and call you back, but you'd gone. So I went to check at the farmhouse."

John took the story up.

"Obviously I was still there. Matt told me what had gone on."

"You realised it was those two men who had sent the note, then?" Sophie asked.

"Well, we guessed. Then we went to tell the adults and got to you as fast as we could. We were a bit quicker than the wrinklies!" laughed John.

"You were just in time! Brilliant tackles!" admired Russell. "Who do you play for?" he asked John.

"I play for a local team usually, I'm Fly Half.

I've just got into the district rugby team, though."

Matthew looked amazed. "Me, too!" he beamed.

"Those two men went down like nine pins. I heard that man's knee pop!" shuddered Sophie.

"I thought it was my shoulder at the time," Matthew said and everyone laughed. Matthew turned to John.

"Thanks," he said and John smiled, reminding everyone of Ben.

The mothers were all waiting patiently when they got back to the campsite.

"We didn't know whether or not to call the police," Mrs Jardine gabbled. "It may not have been an emergency. We didn't know what on earth was going on."

They all listened carefully to what had happened in the last hour and then there was a flurry of activity as they got into cars and drove to the police station.

"I'll just ring Viv," Sophie's mum said, getting out her mobile phone as she sat in the passenger seat.

"She'd kill me if she were to miss this!"

Sergeant Briggs didn't know what had hit him. First of all the dads had tramped into the station with the two criminals, one of them still hobbling quite badly. Then Auntie Viv had arrived. Then all of the mums got there with Sophie, Matthew, Russell and John. It took him a while to sort out exactly what had happened, but even before he'd got the gist of the story, the two men were led through into separate interview rooms.

"Jack Smith and Jamie Thomson," Sergeant Briggs announced. Everyone looked at him, waiting for him to go on.

"You know them?" said Matthew.

"We were looking for them all last night and all of this morning. The Cowlings came in yesterday evening, after all the fire damage and the vandalism that was done to their house. They came back early this morning to make a very interesting statement," the Sergeant said.

Everyone leaned forward to hear better.

"Apparently these two, here, were in the wood at the time of Ben's disappearance. Mr and Mrs Cowling saw them. They've been threatening the Cowlings to keep quiet for years."

"I knew she was hiding something, when we went to see her," Matthew whispered to Russell. The Sergeant went on.

"Apparently, when the story broke about Ben's death, and those two in there read that two men were wanted for questioning, they thought the Cowlings had been in to see us. They hadn't, of course. The Cowlings had realised they would have to come forward, once they'd read the news about Ben in the papers. But they didn't come in to see us and tell us what had been going on until Smith and Thomson had smashed their windows and set fire to the house. The Cowlings guessed it was them, almost straight away. They were really worried about their baby. More worried about his safety than they were scared of the threats Smith and Thomson had been making. Then when we got there, we found evidence to show it definitely was them."

"How?" asked Russell.

"One of the stones they'd thrown through a window," he replied.

"But surely you can't get fingerprints from stones?" said Sophie.

"Not usually, no. But this one was covered in mud. When the mud dried we had a wonderful set of the clearest prints we'd ever seen. Then we just matched them up. We had their prints on record from years ago. A minor poaching offence, but we'd fingerprinted them. Good job. Good job they hadn't even had the sense to wear gloves, thank goodness! So you see, we were closing in on them," said the Sergeant.

"I knew it was them who'd set fire to the Cowling's, too," Sophie piped up. "They let it slip in the wood."

Russell nodded, suddenly realising the significance of what the two men had said about smashing their windows and starting a fire. Sophie's meaningful looks at the time now became clear.

"Well, they'll be thoroughly interviewed. You needn't worry about that. After I've taken statements from you all, you can go home. Well

134

THE WOOD

done all of you, especially you lot!" he smiled at the lads and Sophie.

Chapter 20

Ben's funeral was the day before Bonfire Night, November 4th. It was to be a very quiet affair. Mr and Mrs Walker were determined to keep out the press and say a quiet family goodbye to their son.

Matthew, Russell, Sophie and John had become celebrities almost over night and the press were still hounding them and their families wherever they went.

They had caught two criminals between them and solved the mystery of Ben's disappearance. The police thanked them publicly for their help. They lost count of the number of times they were interviewed and photographed by the press. For a couple of days every newspaper they opened had their own faces printed somewhere inside.

This amused Russell greatly. He cut out the photographs of them all and pasted them into a scrapbook to keep forever, to remind people of when he was famous, or so he said.

Sergeant Briggs had asked them all to call into the police station the day before they had to travel down to the funeral. The four of them had asked to be kept up to date with how the case was going. Sergeant Briggs smiled as they were shown into his office.

"Any news, Sergeant Briggs?" asked Sophie.

The Sergeant nodded.

"Smith told us everything. Thomson too, in the end, but he was the harder nut to crack. A nasty piece of work if you ask me."

"What did they say?" Russell asked.

"Well, apparently, they shot Ben accidentally. They only meant to scare him off. There was an argument over something and Ben went for them."

"They'd been shooting birds," Matthew said simply. "It had annoyed Ben that they'd killed so many and were laughing about it. They were laughing at him too."

Sergeant Briggs frowned and was just about to ask Matthew how on earth he knew all that, when he stopped himself. He decided it was best not to ask. He nodded at Matthew instead.

"You're probably right son," he said. "Anyway, when they realised they'd actually shot him they got scared and ran off when they saw how badly he was bleeding. Then Smith made them go back. Thomson didn't want to. He made that pretty clear in his statement. But Smith was worried. He wanted to make sure Ben was all right. When they found him, though, he was dead. He'd had a bad fall. They saw the gash above his eye, realised he wasn't breathing and panicked. They knew if they had reported it to the police they'd have been in trouble for the shooting. So, stupidly Thomson persuaded Smith that they should bury Ben's body. Smith didn't want to do it, but Thomson told him it was the only way. He was afraid they would be put away for murder you see."

"They should have told the truth," said Sophie, shaking her head. "You would have known Ben had died from the fall, wouldn't you, Sergeant."

"Yes, probably. But the sad fact is that they didn't tell the truth. They buried Ben and hid him well. We made several searches in that wood and didn't come up with a single thing. Ben's bike was the only clue we found and that was only because Smith and Thomson wanted us to find it. They took Ben's bike as far away as they could from his grave."

Matthew, Russell and Sophie exchanged looks.

"We wondered about the bike," said Matthew. "We knew the facts just didn't fit somehow. The bike being found at Stile Copse and all."

Sergeant Briggs nodded. "The best piece of information about the case we got was when the Cowlings came in and gave their statement. The Cowlings had seen them in the wood, just after they had met Ben. Smith and Thomson threatened them, said that they'd better keep quiet if they knew what was good for them. Swore to the couple that they hadn't seen hide nor hair of the lad while they'd been in the wood. The Cowlings knew they had been in trouble with us before and thought the pair of them were trying to keep out of our hair. If only they'd stopped to think why Smith and

Thomson were so desperate for them to keep quiet. If only they'd come forward with the information back then, this case would have been solved a lot more quickly. Smith and Thomson would be inside on lesser charges than they'll face now. Shame really, they dug themselves deeper and deeper into trouble, by not telling the truth and coming clean in the first place."

"Will the Cowlings be in trouble?" asked Matthew.

Sergeant Briggs nodded again.

"They'll have to go to court. Withholding evidence is serious. But there are no special circumstances in this case. I don't think anything drastic is going to happen to them."

"They won't go to prison, will they?" asked Sophie suddenly.

"No, I shouldn't think so, young Sophie," Sergeant Briggs smiled.

"What will Smith and Thomson be charged with?" Matthew had asked.

"Take your pick!" Sergeant Briggs answered. "Failure to inform the coroner of a death, unlawful wounding, threatening behaviour, arson, vandalism, withholding information...it goes on."

"What will they get, do you think?" Russell asked.

"Not sure," shrugged Sergeant Briggs, "but they could get life!"

They all gasped with surprise.

"Justice, though," Matthew said. "They should have told the truth, instead of leaving Ben stuck there, then they wouldn't be in this mess. Justice had to be done."

The others nodded.

On the morning of November 4th they all travelled down to John's house. At eleven o'clock they set off for Ben's funeral. The Jardines had decided not to ride in the funeral procession, behind the hearse with Ben's coffin. It didn't feel quite right.

The church was packed with people when they got there. Young and old. Matthew was surprised to see people even standing around the sides of the church. The service wasn't too morbid either. No one mentioned Ben's death, but talked about celebrating his life. The vicar and close members of Ben's family told lots of stories about all the things he enjoyed doing and what he'd got up to. Funny stories, too, of holidays and Christmasses. Matthew realised even more how much he'd liked Ben and how much like Ben he was. At the end of the service they played Ben's favourite song and everyone filed out, smiling. There were no tears now. He knew Ben would have liked that.

Matthew stood in the churchyard, distanced from the mourners. He half expected to see Ben somewhere about, perhaps behind a tree or near one of the gravestones. But deep down he knew that he'd gone. He had moved on to an adventure that was far more exciting.

John walked over to him and they smiled at each other.

"You all right?" Matthew asked him.

"Yes, thanks. We're all just relieved, I suppose, that we finally got to say a proper goodbye to my brother."

"Yes, he wanted that, too," Matthew said.

"Pardon?" asked John, frowning.

"Sorry, I meant to say, I bet that's what he would have wanted," Matthew corrected himself. "Here, I've been meaning to give you this."

He handed John a paper bag. John took it and looked inside. He pulled out a white handkerchief. It had the initials BW sewn neatly into one of the corners.

"Thanks," said John, "but I've got loads of things to remember him by. You keep it. You found it, it'll be something to remind you of him. Even though you never met him, you must feel as if you know him by now. This hanky must mean a lot to you, after everything you've been through." John smiled, giving the hanky back.

"Yes, thanks, I do know him, in a way," said Matthew, taking the hanky and pushing it into his pocket, gratefully.

Sophie and Russell walked over to them.

"What a lovely service," said Sophie.

"You're sick," mumbled Russell to her. "We've never been to a funeral before, have we Matt."

Matthew glared at his brother and shook his head, nodding over at John at the same time.

John looked down at the floor and mumbled, "Me neither."

"Sorry," Russell apologised quietly.

Auntie Viv suddenly burst in on the group

"By 'eck, me ol' flowers, cheer thyselves up. Do you think Ben would've wanted you standing round wi' faces lookin' as if you'd been suckin' sour lemons? Well?"

No one said anything.

"Are there any words comin' out of my mouth?" she asked, cocking her head to one side. Sophie smiled. Auntie Viv could always cheer her up. She tried to hug them all at once and they found themselves enveloped in a big rugby scrum.

"I'm right proud of you all," she said. "You must all keep in touch, eh? You're a good crowd. Plus, if you come to Soph's, I'll be able to see all thy little faces! Must be off, back to me bit of beef!"

She turned and trotted away from them. She was still wearing her black baseball pumps with black leggings. The rest of her was swathed in an enormous black woollen shawl which smelt of Patchouli oil. Her wild hair flew out behind her as she scuttled to the side of a man and then turned to wave. The man smiled down at her, then looked over to the four of them. Matthew saw the man's smile disappear for a fleeting second as his eyes narrowed.

"Who's that?" Matthew asked Sophie.

"It's Auntie Viv's new boyfriend," she said.

142

"He's an astrologer, or something like that."

"What's one of them, when they're at home?" asked Russell.

"He studies the stars, horoscopes and things like that," Matthew answered.

"Oh, I see. He's staring at you, Matt," Russell nudged him.

"I don't like him," said Matthew.

"How can you say that? You've only just seen him," laughed Sophie. "You've never even met the man." Matthew looked over to him again. The man was still watching him. Suddenly something caught Matthew's eye. He blinked hard, thinking his eyes were playing tricks on him. When he looked again the black shadow he thought he'd seen at the man's right shoulder had vanished. He shivered, then turned his attention back to his friends.

"You will keep in touch?" John said to them all, but especially to Matthew.

"Course!" replied Matthew, "we've got your address. We'll have to meet up during holidays."

"Yes," said John.

"I bet they won't be as exciting as this one!" laughed Russell.

At that moment they were all called back by their parents. John broke away first, and jogged easily back. He gave them a wave.

"See you back at the house," he called.

Matthew, Russell and Sophie walked back slowly, talking as usual.

"It was a lovely service," Sophie said again.

Russell tutted.

"I was surprised at how many people were there," Matthew commented. The other two nodded in agreement.

"I've never seen a church so full," said Russell.

"I know. They were even standing around the sides, up against the walls," Matthew added.

Russell and Sophie looked at one another.

"Don't be daft," Russell laughed uneasily. "All the pews were full. There was no one standing round the sides. No one at all Matthew. I reckon that bump on your head has affected your eyesight."

Matthew stopped dead.

"But..." he began. He frowned. He knew his eyes hadn't deceived him in the church. There were people crammed around the sides of its walls, smiling at all of the stories, nodding their heads and whispering to each other. "Never mind," he said. "Come on, let's get back."

They all ran the last few metres to join their parents. Not one of them looked back, only forward. Forward to whatever adventures lay ahead.